Tìm

THE CENSOR VERSION

By

MICHAEL K. JONES

The Uncensored version is called **Tim**, **The Lost Slave.**

Originally called White Slavery.

CHAPTERS

(TRUE) = Factual History

PROLOGUE

1863

The heavily wooded landscape of northern Georgia seemed to come alive as distant thunder along with flashes of lightning silhouetted trees and bushes for miles. The forest was pitch-black as the noise of fresh falling rain muffled the sounds of quickly moving footsteps. Then suddenly a lightning flash illuminated the wet faces of two running white men and a boy. They came to an exhausting stop and kneeled under the stump of a large fallen tree that dangling enough branches to provide cover from the approaching storm.

"We'll…rest here for a while," gasped the man with a heavily breathing young boy under his arm.

"I haven't seen any railroad tracks," said the other white man. "So where's the *freaken* underground railroad?"

"Sir, please refrain from any colorful metaphors in the presence of my son."

"I'm sorry…my mind has been frequently digressing back to our captors mentality." He then sat sluggishly under a nearby branch. "I've been at that plantation *too* long."

"It is understandable," said the father pitifully looking down at his son. He then reached over and cleared away some dead leaves to expose the soil. "Jonathan, when the rain stops…cover your face and arms with the blackened mud."

"Yes sir," said his red lip son as he cuddled under a partially wet blanket. His father then looked up.

"Tim, we're not catching a train, but following an organized route…to freedom."

****

At the beginning of the 8th century, (740 A.D.) two-hundred years after the fall of the Roman Empire, a conquering army called the Moroccan Moors ruled over the country of Spain for 700 years. The next century, Khazars (white people) from the Caucasus region of Russia migrated south to

Israel and began converting the Hebrew religion into their own, they call today as Judaism. Later, those same Jewish imposters, under the disguise of the Dutch East India Company, financed a percentage of ships that sailed captured Hebrew slaves, some they also owned, to the America's from the 1600's to the 1850's. (TRUE)

It is an on-going debate as to whether the nomadic Moors were so-called Black *Israelites* or *Hamite* Arabs. They did successfully conquer parts of northern Africa, southern Italy, and the island of Crete. There, they developed a taste for white women, enslaving a multitude of them for their own sexual pleasures. (True) Spaniards and Italians to this day will deny their genetic link to Africans even as the evidence of proof is in their curly black hair and light beige skin. Maybe this is why they called it, *The Dark Ages*.

As time passed, when the Moroccan Moors were slowly forced out of the Iberian Peninsula, they were responsible, including the Africans and Assyrian Arabs, for the capturing and selling of exiled Hebrew *Israelites* (The lost Tribe of Judah) to the Europeans who shipped them to America. (TRUE)

Well in this book, a white man named Arthur C. Wellington experienced a different world. The so-called Black Hebrews, who disliked their captors, reverse engineered a captured Spanish Galleon and built three sailing vessels of their own. The first completed Hebrew built ship to arrive in America was called the מייפל אואר, landing on *Plymouth Rock* before the British who left England to escape religious persecution. They were forced to sail the Mayflower 2 further north, landing on the shores of Nova Scotia which is now Canada.

Over time, America became a so-called Black nation which economically grew, thanks to the enslavement of white post Anglo Saxons who were captured from the impoverished country of England. The Moors and Arabs hired the Irish and some disloyal locals to capture white British citizens including some Scottish from the north, and ship them to the new world (America) where they were to be auctioned off to the highest bidders.

Story References

The Dark Ages was between the 5th and 15th centuries.

Amalek: Esau's grandson.

Esau: Older son of Isaac in the Hebrew Bible who was born with red skin. (white people)

Edomite: Ancient (white) people from the kingdom of Edom.

Hamite: People of Africa not related to the Israelites. Descendants of Ham, Noah's son.

מייפל אואר: In Hebrew means Mayflower.

Ouidah: means Whydah or Judah. Name of slave trade city in Benin, Africa.

The 12 Lost tribes of Israel.
(There is no 13th tribe for the Jewish imposters in Israel)
So-called

Judah: (Black Americans)

Reuben: (Seminole Indians)

Simeon: (Dominicans)

Levi: (Haitians)

Ephraim: (Puerto Ricans)

Naphtali: (Argentina to Chile)

Asher: (Columbia to Uruguay)

Issachar: (Mexicans)

Zebunun: (Guatemala to Panama)

Benjamin: (West Indians)

Manasseh: (Cubans)

Gad: (N. Americans Indians)

CHAPTER 1

The Voyage/Isaiah 14:2

"My name is *not* Tim, it's Arthur C. Wellington the third."

"Please except my apology. I'm Winston Cartney and this is my son Jonathan. He was to be sold tomorrow and this was our only chance to escape."

"I thank you for your hospitality in letting me accompany you and your son."

"Get some rest. The black *Hunter-Gatherers* will be alerted of our escape in the morning, that's after the overseers do a roll call."

"Thank God," said Arthur. "Because those eyes and teeth galloping in the darkness, scares the *crap* of me." The father silently frowned at him. "I meant...bowel movement."

The rain began to ease as Arthur closed his eyes, fearing to go to sleep. At twenty-two years old, he still recalled clearly the day he was taken away from his home and country. The light rain that pelted his head seemed to simultaneously fall on the bricked streets that his mind recalled. The dark wet buildings gave off a glow of despair as people were not seen on the streets after sun down. One particular night, Arthur's parents sensed what everybody in the town felt.

"Fear," whispered Tim as he rubbed one of the wet bleeding cuts caused by the ankle shackles he squeezed his feet through. Then he recalled the one noise that his mother feared the most. It was the sound of a horse drawn carriage speeding down the empty streets of London. She was told stories of how whole families were captured and never to be heard from again. It was rumored that the *darkies* across the ocean had a taste for white meat.

"Be extremely quiet Arthur."

"Yes Mother," he said with an English accent. The both of them were hiding in the largest closet in the farthest back room. Arthur's dad had left earlier that day to secure three seats on a vessel sailing for France.

"Mother, when is Father coming home?"

"Quiet." Then a loud sound was heard as three men burst into the house. A minute later, the closet door swung open as Arthur's mother screamed.

"Wench, shut the frack up!" said a large white man with an Irish accent and curly red hair. "Is that a leprechaun?" Arthur began to cry as the smelly man lifted him up and licked his face. "This young lad will get us a hefty sum." His two partners, both disloyal locals grabbed his mother and pulled her out of the closet.

"Mother!" yelled Arthur as the men dragged her into another room while un-buckling their belts and then slamming the door shut. It was the last time Arthur saw his mother as he was carried by the Irishman like a stray dog, then thrown into a cage at the back of a two horse drawn carriage. He cried in agony as he reached through the bars toward his bricked home, the rain blending in with his tears.

Three hours later, he was placed on a large sailing vessel one deck down and shackled by the neck to a lonely round support column that rose from the floor to the ceiling. The level was dark and hot as the smell of sweat and urine filled the air. Shirtless overweight white men were hand-shackled together wrist to wrist and forced to wear old shredded knee-high pants. They sat on the deck floor, some leaning against each other shoulder to shoulder with their legs spread apart. It was there that Arthur saw his true captors.

"Excuse me Sir…excuse me," shouted Arthur to get a tall dark skinned man's attention. "I would like to protest my incarceration under these deplorable conditions and *demand* my immediate release."

"Shut up *Esau*…before I eat you."

These people do think I'm food, possibly filet mignon. Arthur's thoughts then turned to fear. *Mother was right…these chosen people are going cook my legs and arms. And what the heck is a Esau?*

The ship sailed two hours later, after a large cargo of crates and barrels were stored onboard. Arthur assumed the crates were filled with carrots, potatoes, and the barrels, topped-off with wine for the feast that was going to occur after they reached their destination.

The next day, the sun rose brightly when Arthur was awakened to the smell of something delicious. *Oh no...the darkies have begun the cannibalistic feast.* He then looked toward the stern to see what white men were missing, and his eyes opened wide. The hand shackled men were being fed a breakfast fit for a king.

"You slaves better eat all this slop!" yelled one of the three Hebrew cooks.

They're just fattening us up. Thought Arthur as he watched all the white men eating like hungry pigs. He tried to stand up to see if there was a black, man size steel cauldron nearby. *There has to be a reason for this feast.* He thought seeing nothing. One brown skinned cook walked up to him with a plate of scrambled cheese eggs, turkey bacon, and a metal cup of orange juice.

"Sit your skinny butt down." Arthur sat quickly as the man placed the plate of food in front of him. Arthur just looked at it. "What's your problem?" asked the angry looking cook.

"I'm not hungry," said Arthur.

"Why, this food isn't good enough for you?"

"These conditions, along with the sea air, and the rocking of this vessel has curbed my appetite." The cook kneeled down, grabbed a handful of eggs, and shoved them into Arthur's mouth.

"How's that taste wigger?"

"It's delicious," mumbled Arthur.

"Skinny white boys are not profitable...and I'll feed your butt every day if you don't eat. You hear what I'm saying?"

"Not really," he responded while chewing.

"Are you getting smart with me?"

"No...sir, I just don't understand your language."

"Edomite it's English!"

Arthur remained quiet thinking the man was emotionally disturbed. Then a familiar fishy smell hit his nose. *That belligerent Hamite resembling Negro smells like grandma, after taking a dump.*

The ship was three weeks into its two month voyage when the deck came alive with excitement. The captive men were cheering and screaming as one of them, a sickly thin red face white Esau had escaped from his hand shackles. He had run up from the deck below, trying to reach the top. Arthur excitingly recognized him.

"Father!" he yelled.

"Arthur...*Arthur* is that really you?"

"Yes." His dad then ran to him and gave him a hug.

"Where's your mother?"

"The red heads have her."

"I was captured at the dock," said his father. "The vessel sailing to France was a lie...only to lure me to this ship."

"Where are they taking us?" asked Arthur.

"To America."

"Are they going to eat us?"

"They're going to sell us and then make us breed with their mothers."

"Ain't I too young?" asked Arthur. At that moment two so-called Black shipmates with whips tried to corner his father.

"I'm *not* for sale!" shouted Arthur's dad. "I'm only having intercourse with *my* wife!" He then ran past his angry captors as fast as a Muslim jogging through a pig farm and then up the steps to the main deck. A minute later after hearing foul words as the chase ensued; Arthur heard his father's last words.

"Freedom!" yelled his dad before hitting the ocean water. It was the only word branded into Arthur's mind for the rest of his life, including the horrifying screams his dad made when the sharks started taking bites out of him.

16th Century Painting (Lisbon Portugal)
(TRUE)
YouTube search **(The Black Hebrew Inquisition Part 1-3)** and watch video.
Google (Moorish Jews of Portugal)

In the 1480's during the Spanish Inquisition, thousands of Black Jews were deported back to West Africa. It is also documented that the so-called black *Hebrew Inquisition* began in 1492, and parents that did not convert to Christianity had their children 3 to 10 years old sent alone to Guinea Africa.

CHAPTER 2

The Arrival

Almost two months into the voyage, the ship experienced its first storm. Its intensity caused the ship to shutter and gyrate as its wooden frame seemed to bend in and outward, scaring the involuntary subdued passengers. Most of them moaned uncontrollably as the cold salt water irritated their newly formed butt sores. Arthur could see fear in the eyes of the wet hand shackled men that were near to him. He also could hear some crying as their wet overlapping bellies seem to clap against each other. It was then, at that very moment, he wanted death to take him. He had lost his mother and father, and had nothing to live for.

"White Jesus, I beseech you to take me from this vessel!" he cried with his eyes closed tightly. "Take me *Cesare*…please!" The rocking of the ship induced vomiting on all three decks and Arthur knew it would reduce the farting of some nearby captives that made him nauseous. It was about ten minutes later when the storm seemed to dissipate causing the sun to forcefully shine through the receding clouds. Arthur then realized his prayers weren't going to be answered and he would have to finish the voyage.

Later that night as the moonlight partially lit the deck through the portholes, snoring and farting echoed again throughout the entire ship. Arthur was awakened not by the snoring, but by a single white man crying. He was causing the others close to him to also awaken, and then he saw a sight that was disturbing to him. Another white captive next to the crying man shoved his face deep into his lap and began suckling him like a hungry puppy.

I'm thirsty too. Thought Arthur. *But not for urine*. It seemed to work because the man stopped crying and the other awakened captives also offered, some demanding to relinquish their urine to the thirsty shipmate.

The next day, the sun rose to a chilly morning as the captured sleeping white men were huddled together like fallen dominoes to keep warm. The ship then rattled to the sound of wood hitting wood. It was resting at a dock and fear fell again upon the faces of all the captured men. They knew they would be eaten alive that night or killed, possibly stored in barrels of salt to preserve their meat. Arthur was more afraid as he shivered in fear at the same intensity the night he was taken from his mother. *I am the first to be eaten*. He thought as thirty to forty large dark skinned men entered the ship on all three decks.

Screams of horror echoed throughout the vessel as the white men were pulled like a tug-o-war, some dragged while falling on the splintered deck of the ship. Arthur was unlocked from his lonely spot and kicked as he struggled to get up to walk. He knew he was being tenderized and came to terms of his eminent demise. Arthur reached the upper deck and the sun's glare blinded him as he was unable to see where he was going. "Move your little *Amalek* red face!" yelled the so-called Black man as he kicked him again while holding a chain leashed to his neck shackle. Arthur struggled to move as he heard awful sounds of newly captured slaves, some crying women. He was unaware of them being on the ship and *hope* filled his heart, thinking his mother was also onboard. His blurred vision was slowly returning as the sounds of his captors seem to come from the top of horses.

"Let's move these wenches into the auction house!" shouted an older nappy white haired man on top of a horse. Arthur rubbed his eyes, hoping to see the women. They were screaming and some crying as they were being pulled by their wrist shackles. Arthur squinted like a Japanese crackhead trying to see if his mother was in the line as the women entered into a large wooden building. He did not see her and his heart was once again heavy with disappointment, wishing to be seasoned and barbequed with an apple in his mouth.

A forty year old white female in a clean off-white dress was ordered to take him separately to a different building as the white men were dragged into the same building with the women.

"Ma'am, are you one of the cooks?" asked Arthur.

"No lad…I'm just going to get you cleaned up."

"When am I to be eaten?"

"What are you talking about?"

"My mother said, the Negro's like white meat and we are to be eaten."

"No…you are to be sold and then maybe work on a plantation."

"You're not seasoning me for their dinner?"

"I'm going to wash and cloth you for the auction."

"Do I still have to *have* intercourse with mothers?"

"Hush with the silly questions and no…just be quiet."

Twenty minutes later, Arthur was clean and dressed in an old red colonial *Livery* boys dress suit. Then he was escorted to a large open stage that seated numerous wealthy so-called Black men in the audience. An announcement was made and he was the first to be auctioned off.

"The bidding on this little fart starts at five dollars." The men began to shout out words he didn't understand as the price seemed to get higher.

"Going once, going twice," shouted the auctioneer looking toward the bidders. Then a real dark skinned man entered the auction area wearing a large brim hat. He looked like a so-called black Clint Eastwood with big lips.

"I'll double that price!" he yelled as the auctioneer then smiled. Arthur became scared as the tall man stood confidently while hungrily picking his teeth with a long piece of pine straw.

I'm definitely going to be eaten. Thought Arthur. *That spook looks hungry*.

"Any takers?" asked the auctioneer looking around as the seating area became silent. "Timmy is yours—pay the clerk in the back."

"Who is Timmy?" asked Arthur. A stagehand reattached a neck shackle and yanked him to the wooden floor.

"Shut up *Edomite*," he shouted at Arthur. He then pulled him off the stage as the buyers cheered when a young naked white woman with red hair was brought out for sale.

An hour later, Arthur was placed in the back of an open uncovered wagon with two older white women. It was driven by a middle-aged white slave that looked like a constable from his hometown.

"Excuse me kind gentleman…excuse me," said Arthur to get his attention. "Where are you taking us?"

"Quiet before *Master* hears you."

"I just want to know, if I'm to be eaten tonight?" The white man softly laughed as he shook the horse reigns up and down to increase the wagon's speed.

"When you get a little older, Miss Maple might eat you—she loves some white meat."

"Oh no…I knew it," said Arthur. The white man smiled as Master James pulled further ahead on his saddled horse.

"I was eaten last week," said the horse driver with a smile.

Three hours later, they passed through a side gate in the back of the plantation, and witnessed a white man being whipped in front of ten other white male slaves who were ordered to watch. The wagon passed the moaning slave as his hands were rope tide to two vertically standing logs. He was slumped over as his back bled like dripping red paint. The two so-called Black overseers (supervisors who were in charge of all the white slaves on the plantation) were taking turns whipping him, playing tic-tac-toe on his back as blood oozed over the black charcoal marked squares.

"Why is that constituent being thrashed?" Arthur asked the wagon driver who began to smile.

"He willfully refused to acknowledge his new name."

"And what was that name?" asked Arthur.

"Tyrone."

"I'm keeping my name."

"Your new name is Tim and you better answer to it," said the wagon driver.

"I am…that whip looks bacterially infectious."

The wagon driver chuckled while shaking the reigns. He then stopped at the back side of the plantation in front of a waiting darker skinned white foreman. Tim noticed a row of white houses with white picket fences. "Your new name is Tim," said the foreman.

"Why?" asked Arthur believing he was Italian.

"Because wigger...Master James said so!" shouted the agitated foreman. "And you better not use that word *why* ever again."

"What's a wigger?"

"Your pale white inbred little butt."

"I'm a wigger based on my skin color?"

"We are *all* wiggers."

"I'm British," said Tim with his chin up.

"You're a dummy who doesn't have a country anymore," said the foreman. "You are now a wigger that's the property of Master James."

"I won't be forever."

"Are you eye-balling me boy?"

"I'm only conversing with you and eye contact is a respectful response."

"Don't you ever look any Israelites directly in their eyes...or your butt will get bullwhipped."

Tim fought himself to *not* ask why as they walked to his new sleeping quarters. He was then handed some soft cotton hand-me-down clothes worn by a slave boy who was recently whipped to death. Tim couldn't resist and asked the foreman one more important question.

"Why are we all here against our will?"

"We are here to help Master James make money. And in return…he takes care of us."

"I don't want to stay here—can I leave?"

"You can never leave," said the foreman. "You are to work in the fields until Master James decides otherwise."

"What do they grow in the fields?"

"A plant that is inhaled in large quantities."

"Tobacco?" asked Arthur.

"No, this plant makes you hungry."

"I don't want any of that—I'm already hungry."

"The buffet begins at six o'clock."

"I don't have a watch."

"When you hear a bell ring…its supper time."

"I'm hearing bells now."

CHAPTER 3

Apple Pie

Tim fell asleep after his daydream and awakened to the sound of a distant noise. The rain had stopped and he was alone in the woods realizing the increasing sound *was* a bell. Winston Cartney and his son were gone as the galloping of horses in his direction increased in volume.

The *Hunter-Gatherers* rang a bell to flush out runaways hiding in the woods. Tim didn't know this and ran as fast as he could. The sun was rising and he became angry at the other white slave for leaving him to be captured. *I'm going to be spotted like bear crap in winter snow.* He then remembered the man rubbing mud on the face of his son. He stopped near a trench next to a tree and buried himself under the wet mulch of dead leaves. Three minutes later, the horses galloped past him and he decided to stay there till night fall. He took naps and often heard the sounds of nearby animals breathing. Then he became wet with warm urine he believed was from a male white-tailed deer marking its territory. He didn't care because he was not moving until it was completely dark outside.

Two hours before sunset, he heard the same number of horses heading his way from the opposite direction. They had captured his deserting white companion and his son. They made him walk all the way back to the plantation as they dragged him by a rope tied around both of his hands. His son, with mud still on his face, rode side-saddle with the *Hunter-Gatherer* who dragged his father.

"Slugface keep up!" shouted the slave hunter. "Before I shoot your lily white butt in front of your son." The escaped slave was exhausted and out of breath as he was being pulled.

Tim waited till the sky was completely dark, and then ran in the direction of the *North Star*. Every white slave in captivity knew to follow the handle of the *Little Dipper* star cluster. It was said, it would lead them to freedom, to the northern Confederate States that didn't agree with white slavery in America. He knew that if he made it to North Virginia, he would no longer be considered a slave. If the rumors he heard were true, he was going to join the Northern Confederate Army and help free his people from slavery.

Tim rose from under the mulch as the stench of urine was more potent. He needed to find a stream or river as hunger hindered his stride in the darkness of night. *I'm a dead man if I don't wash this smell off.* He thought hearing a coyote howl in the distance. The sky became clouded as the view of the *Little Dipper* disappeared. He continued in the same direction and thank God for what happened next. It started raining again and he heard the sounds of something falling out of a tree ahead of him. It was apples as he also heard fearful deer's galloping away. He ate like the men on the slave ship, shoveling two apples into his face with both hands. After finishing them, he filled both his pockets with smaller apples and continued his quest northward. An hour later, he rested near a stream thinking about the day he first tasted apple pie. He was thirteen and assigned as a kitchen servant. Master James's wife, Miss Maple had just painfully walked down the stairs in a beautiful black dress that was too small for her huge waistline. She was darker than the dress as her eye-catching red lipstick only added to her ugliness.

"You're looking lovely today Madam," lied the head servant who wore a white tuxedo with black gloves. He held up a polished silver tray toward her with two lemon topped glasses of tea. He was ordered to lie everyday and dreaded his turn to be eaten. She took one glass and tipped it up, drinking it non-stop until it was empty. She then exerted a horrifying burp like a hippo farting under water.

Damn! Tim shouted in his mind as he heard the burp from the kitchen. *Nasty whore*. It was then, at that very moment, he realized he was losing his heritage. He knew he was unwillingly being indoctrinated into his captors culture. *That's just freaken great—I'm a Black American.*

Dinner was being served when Master James entered the dining room. The long, hand carved *Cherry wood* dining room table was full of food; corn bread, fried chicken, chitterlings, collard greens smothered in pigs-feet, and macaroni and cheese topped off with a boiled pig tongue that sat next to two smoldering hot apple pies. Tim stared at the food and almost regurgitated his roast beef on rye sandwich he had eaten for lunch. He couldn't understand how they ate that food as he hovered over one of the apple pies. *I would love to try some of that.* He thought knowing he could be horse-whipped. He then took a fork and carefully dug under the pie crust to taste the filling. It was a taste he had never experienced, and almost had an orgasm in his white tuxedo. He cleaned the fork, and then left the dining area as Master James and his wife entered to eat dinner. They made themselves a plate and sat in the den. Tim always wondered why they ate there and not in the dining room. Nobody knew why.

After dinner, Miss Maple wanted something sweet and decided to cut herself a piece of pie.

She noticed it was dug into and became very angry. "Dauntay!" she yelled. The head servant ran to her and stood nervously looking toward the floor, never making eye contact. "Did you eat this pie?"

"No Madam." She became furious as she wobbled into the kitchen with the pie in her hand. She then had all the kitchen staff line up in front of the stove, later ordering the women to leave.

"Who *ate* some of this apple pie?" she asked sternly. "I said…who the *frack* ate my pie?" There was no answer as Tim's skinny knees began to buckle. "Okay," she said knowing one of the two white female slaves could have eaten it. "Since nobody knows who ate this pie…all of you will be eating pie tonight. Be at my bedroom door at eight o'clock."

"It was me," shouted Dauntay, the head servant. "I should be whipped for my insolence."

"Oh…no," she said shaking her finger. "You're eating more pie tonight and it's itching to be licked."

Why did he sacrifice himself? Tim asked himself. *She has a big hairy pie under that dress.* He then felt remorseful, but not stupid. *Maybe he likes getting bullwhipped or eating hot smelly vagina.*

Later that night, after Master James left the plantation for the weekend, moans from his wife were heard all across the plantation as coyotes returned her calls of the wild, howling in response.

****

Tim had fallen asleep again as the scratching of mosquito bites woke him from a deep slumber. He forgot to rub more *Bloodroot* leafs on his arms and legs he picked earlier. It was discovered by the local Indians as a natural repellent against numerous insects. He knew the best time for escaping was just before spring, before the bugs returned. It was mid-summer and the only time he could escape from that God-awful plantation.

Tim ate another apple and felt better after drinking from a fresh-water stream. He then ran like the speed of a chariot as trees blurrily past him as he maintained a steady stride. The thirst of freedom was his motivation as he came upon the same dirt road he heard about from captured runaway slaves. He then remembered a white slave named Trey who had his foot cut off for escaping more than four times. Trey had overheard a *Hunter-Gatherer* say a slave got away by following the red road northward. He told every white male slave about the red road that lead to freedom.

Tim could taste freedom, thanking God for helping him find the red-clay road. It was his guide from now on. He carefully followed the dirt road while constantly stopping and looking at his callous foot. *It looks like a familiar menstruating vagina I ate.* Then he heard the sound of galloping horses heading south in his direction and quietly ducked behind a bush. He listened to voices of men saying that they won a lot of battles and the enemy was retreating. Tim stood up suddenly after they passed. *Those were black Southern Union soldiers.* Speculating they were patrol scouts and warning that evil General Grannt that the Confederate north was advancing southward.

Don't worry Mr. Dauntay…your pie eating days are almost over. He thought while visualizing the faces of the old abused servants at the plantation. *And no more cigars that squirt a money shot in Mrs. Glenda's face.*

Three days later, Tim finally reached the end of the red road. He sneezed and then coughed as he came into view of a large field, noticing smoke rising from the northern side. "It's the *Grey Coats*," he shouted as he began to excitingly run. *Free at last…free at last…thank President Lee, I'm free at last.* In one split second, a frown of fear suddenly fell upon his face. He was ambushed by a couple of so-called Black southern Union soldiers who were waiting in the bushes for the Confederates to pass.

"And where the frack did you come from wigger?" The other Union soldier stood up from the bushes, holding his musket rifle.

"Quietly kill him and get back over here." At that moment a large group of so-called Black northern Confederate soldiers on horseback galloped in their direction. The southern soldier pulled Tim at gunpoint into the bushes while holding his mouth in silence. He had caught a cold and almost sneezed through the soldier's fingers.

After being escorted for miles, Tim had no idea he was about to be drafted into the southern Union Army. They took him back to their base camp where he was given an oversized Union uniform and no rifle. He was ordered to be a servant for General Shermane and his senior officers who were planning a massive offensive attack.

CHAPTER 4

Breakfast

"Just dandy," whispered Tim as he walked with a tray of coffee and tea toward the tent of the biggest so-called Black General he had ever seen.

I'm a traitor to my own race if I kill just one Confederate northerner. He then coughed up some thick green phlegm. *I should be in the northern army and killing these slavery sympathizers.* He walked into the General's tent as a light skinned guard at his post angrily eyeballed him.

"Sir…would you like coffee or tea?"

"I'll have coffee, but first." The General leaned back in his wooden chair, looking past Tim. "Guard!" he yelled. The guard ran in and stood at attention. "Drink this tea," he ordered.

"Yes Sir," said the guard picking up the metal cup. He took a big sip of the smoldering tea, and then the General waited. He wanted to make sure it wasn't poisoned. "Back to your post."

"Yes Sir," said the guard almost running. The General then grabbed the hot coffee mug and began sipping. Tim left the tent smiling. *It's poisoned...with phlegm and mucus.* He smiled while wondering if the guard swallowed all of his slime. *Those two will feel like shit in a couple of days.*

That night, he was moved from sleeping on the ground, to sharing a tent with two other white slaves who were forced to fight for the south. They also hated the southern so-called Blacks, and would even tolerate the northern darkies if they could escape to the north. One white slave did live in Boston before the war.

"Tell me...what's it like up north?" asked Tim as he sat around a camp fire with three other white slaves. Tyrese took a sip of his hot tea, and then looked at each of them.

"The women are real friendly, especially at night."

"Are you talking about the Hebrew women?" ask Tim.

"Yeah…they act all proper and dress pretty in the Sabbath day time, but at night…when they get a little liquor in their system, they get crazy."

"How do you know this?" asked another white slave.

"I was washing dishes in the back of this fried chicken and waffle restaurant, and this large big butt…dark chocolate woman made a wrong turn while looking for a toilet."

"They do have big extremities," said Tim thinking about Miss Maple while sneezing."

"Why do you talk like that?" asked another white slave looking directly at Tim.

"I'm holding on to my heritage even under the unfavorable conditions bestowed upon me in this country."

"Your crazy butt better get with the times…you're not in the promised-land anymore."

"Shut the funk up and let me tell this story," shouted Tyrese. "She was so drunk…I told her to use this bucket because the out-house around back was occupied. That woman pulled up her skirt in front of me…showing her hairy nappy snatch, and pissed so hard, her booty and dress were dripping wet."

"That wasn't so crazy."

"Later that night…she ate buttered rice and fried chicken," said Tyrese. "Except…the restaurant ran out of butter early that morning."

"You're the crazy son-of-a-goat," said the pale white slave next to Tim.

"Retribution is unnecessary when we stoop to the levels of our captors," stated Tim.

"Wigger please!" shouted Tyrese. "I saw when you added that extra mouth crème to the General's coffee."

"That woman was a civilian," said Tim. "The General isn't."

"You're nuts," said Tyrese.

Tim then stood up. "I'm turning in for the night," he said angrily. He left the campfire and decided he was going to escape under the cover of night. He later sneaked out the back of his tent and left his dark blue infantry jacket rolled up with piled up dirt and grass under his blanket. It gave an impression he was asleep. Tim could still hear the white slaves giggling as Tyrese told another unbelievable story."

"Are you sure...*you* weren't jerking yourself off?" another slave asked Tyrese.

"Kesha (Big Butt) Billows was her name, and she was a college fresh-men attending Harvard. She had a thing for white meat and I was...at the right place, at the right time."

"She must've been pretty drunk," said another slave.

"She was," said Tyrese. "And at first, she thought I was a half white malato named Derek. That night, I was going to be anybody she wanted me to be."

"You could've been hung if you were caught."

"Speaking of hung...she said I wasn't." The men began to laugh out loud.

Tim left the campsite after rubbing his face and entire upper body with burnt, black tree amber. He had stolen it from the previous night's campfire. His black face, body, and the color of his dark blue uniform pants helped him slip past all the patrols that guarded the Union campsite. He didn't want to kill any soldiers that were fighting for his people's freedom, so desertion was his only option. He knew he could be shot if he was recaptured, but he had to take that chance.

The other white slaves probably will be tortured because I escaped. He thought while walking through the woods. *Who cares...they were blue-eyed devils anyway.* Tim felt no remorse as he continued northward.

Four hours later, he was leaning against a tree and fell into a dream like state, reminiscing about last month and how he ended up in the woods. He recalled, it was his last day as being a house wigger. He was assigned to the fields because Master James was too cheap to buy more white slaves to harvest the crops. It was still the happiest and the most unforgettable day of his life.

****

A covered wagon had entered through the plantation's main gate as he spotted it from the hot, muggy field. Master James met the wagon on horseback and jumped off. A so-called Black man on the reigns walked to the back of the wagon and ordered seven white women to jump off.

Is that? Tim asked himself. *No...it can't be?* "Mother!" he screamed as he began to run from the field. A joy had filled his heart as he saw his mother's butt being fondled by Master James. Then without warning, he blacked out. He was shot by a *Hunter-Gatherer's* musket who thought he was escaping.

Tim woke up three days later with a high fever. His bullet wound was infected as blood soaked white bandages covered the hole in his right shoulder. He was sweating and when he opened his eyes, all he remembered was calling for his mother. "Where's my mother?" he asked lethargically.

"Tim, your mother is gone," said Shanequa, a middle-aged white woman who took care of all the slaves when they were sick.

"I saw her...near the wagon."

"Stay calm…you have a fever," she said rinsing a bloody white rag in water. "That was a traveling whorehouse, mainly for lonely single plantation owners."

"Master James isn't single."

"That woman at the main-house…is his sister."

"Oh…that explains why she gives away pie."

"And *why* don't you like it?" asked Shanequa while placing another wet rag on his forehead. "You kept screaming that you hate eating apple pie."

"Do you know where the wagon travels?"

"I heard it…just started traveling from New Orleans and will circle back from South Carolina. It may come back in about three weeks." Tim laid on the bed with his arm in a sling, sweating like a live pig at a bacon processing plant. He just stared blindly up in the air at the wooden ceiling. "You still haven't answered my question?" she asked.

"That woman makes the servants eat her pie," Tim said a little angry.

"Did it taste bad?"

"Indeed…and it's covered with barb-wire."

"What are you talking about?"

Tim was tired of talking as Shanequa thought he was delusional from the fever. She left the slave cabin as Tim's heart was filled with hope. He knew why God didn't take his life on the slave ship...because his mother was still alive. He had a motivation to escape the plantation again, and one day be reunited with her.

Tim's fever had broken and he couldn't work the fields with one arm so Master James assigned him back to the house. He cleaned dishes and sometimes at dinner time, carried trays of food with one hand to the table. He was happy until one weekend had changed his life.

It was a Saturday morning when his lifetime of nightmares began. Before the sun had risen, Tim was called to the kitchen by the head house *wigger,* to prepare breakfast. It was predicted that Master James loved to eat cheese-grits, eggs, and fried pork-fat on the weekends, especially on Saturday mornings. The house crew started early, preparing breakfast in the same orderly fashion until unexpectedly, Miss Maple called for help.

The kitchen foreman ordered Tim to go up to her aid and he declined mentally, dreading the selfish woman.

"Please white Jesus…don't let her make me eat pie for breakfast?" whispered Tim while walking up the long curved stairway to the second floor. He then knocked softly on her door.

"Get your butt in here!" she yelled. Tim knew it wasn't her pie eating voice. He opened the door and it was worst. Miss Maple's was completely naked with her huge dark skinned titties hanging under both arm pits. She was wet with sweat as the fluffy nappy hair between her legs glistened like Michael Jackson's *Jheri-curls* just before it caught on fire. "Get over here and help me." Tim walked quickly, but hindered his steps slightly enough not to be noticed. He was scared as he got closer to the bed. She then threw a dirty towel at him and struggled with two hands to lift one of her huge oversized black nipple breast. It exposed a forming puddle of sweat underneath it. "Wipe under this heavy son-of-a biscuit." Tim began to cry internally as he used his good hand and wiped in a clock wise motion. The smell was unbearable, like skunk piss mixed with tuna fish, spread across a moose's nuts. She began to strain from the weight as Tim feared she might let go and smother him to death. That very moment was worst than eating pie as he walked around the bed, ignoring the large opening between her legs that he knew so well. Tim then wiped the crater under the other large titty as her morning breath and unwashed sweaty body caused his left eye to uncontrollably twitch. "This hot summer heat is killing me," she said after dropping her breast like wet hamburger hitting a hot skillet.

"Yes Ma'am," agreed Tim not really caring. She then grabbed a flowered Spanish hand fan and opened her legs wider. Tim threw up in his mouth.

"Bring your face over here," she demanded as the look of fear intensified on his face.

"Ma'am, I...I have a injured arm and have to prepare the morning breakfast. Master James will be angry if we're late."

"Get your skinny rectum out of here," she said angrily while trying to reach past one of her huge breast to fan her crotch. "You're eating some pie tonight." That was Tim's signal to form a plan of escape before that fat heifer served him desert.

After breakfast, he stole as much food as he could without getting caught. Later that day, the foreman was bull-whipped for the missing food. Tim was kind of glad because he sent him upstairs to help that fat nasty woman with the glandular problem.

Before sunset, he attempted his first escape and was caught within an hour. Even though he didn't eat pie, he was whipped with five lashes and his feet shackled together for two months.

I would've accepted ten lashes. He thought after his shackles were removed. *For not having to lick that unwashed beaver trap that oozed chlamydian juice down her butt crack.*

CHAPTER 5

I'm Back

Tim's head was resting against the tree as drool revived him from his deep slumber after his reminiscing day-dream. It was morning as he got up feeling dizzy and a little warmer than normal. He sluggishly continued northward knowing he was getting sick again.

Later, around noontime, he crossed over a rocky hill and spotted a caged slave wagon with newly arrived whites being transported westward. Then he heard the cannon fire of a large battle being fought. He decided to discretely visit a nearby town and hopefully find someone willing to give him some food. He knew his odds were slim as the battle grew in intensity. He saw a white man and woman running in the opposite direction. They looked like recent runaways as he tried to catch up to them.

"Excuse me!" he yelled to get their attention. They glanced in his direction, not slowing their run. "Why are you heading west?" The female looked at him strangely as she slowed her pace.

"You better hide," she shouted. "The Union soldiers will shoot you on sight." Tim then believed the southern Army must be winning the war and are advancing north.

"We are heading northwest," shouted the man grabbing the female's hand to quicken her steps.

"What's out west?" asked Tim.

"Friendly *Moolies* with straight black hair," said the woman. Tim had heard about the natives that were driven from their Canadian land up north many years ago.

"I wouldn't trust them…they have the skin color of our masters." The couple looked at him strangely and continued westward.

Tim decided to use the woods for cover and go around the town. He spotted a one horse wagon speeding with two thin Hebrew females heading in his direction near the tree line. They both were wearing long dresses with 613 fringed tassels at the bottom. One woman shook the reigns as the other held an umbrella to shield her dark skin from the blistering sun. Tim noticed the wagon was carrying army supplies, but a basket of fruits and vegetables is what got his attention. *I'm going to confiscate that basket.* He thought only motivated by his hunger. *They're just jezebels with food for the enemy.* He jumped out the woods into the middle of the road and screamed like a *Hamite* Zulu warrior running into battle. The wagon swirled a little to the right, but didn't lose its speed as he jumped on top of the reigned horse, to get it to stop.

The black as tar female holding the umbrella reached behind her and pulled up a slave master's bullwhip. She popped that thing twice before hitting Tim on his back. He screamed like a caged monkey with an anal infection as the pain he remember from previous whippings, shot through his entire body. He opened his eyes while reaching behind his back, and he was back at the plantation, in the cannabis field as Master James snapped the whip back while on his horse.

"Get your sick butt back to work," he yelled. Tim thought he was dreaming and needed to wake up. He was hijacking a wagon and the next second, he was back on the plantation that grew a special tobacco for people with no appetites.

This is a fracking nightmare. He thought picking leaves from the vines while looking around bewildered and confused. *I hope this is a dream*. He pinched himself to try and wake up as other field slaves stared at him. The white women started pinching themselves, some twisting their nipples while laughing out loud. Tim looked down and knew he had escaped, seeing that the scars on his shackled feet were healed. It was the time he lost, he couldn't remember. *What happened that caused me to forget*? He asked himself over and over.

Later that day, when he returned to his newly assigned slave cabin he shared with three other slaves, he asked Demetrius one question. "In these difficult times, I am at a loss of words to describe my present dilemma. I have somehow lost…maybe mentally, forgotten a period of time in my life." Tim paused in thought as Trayvon jumped in his bunk. "How...did I arrive at this establishment?"

"By fracking boat!" shouted Eddie, the oldest roommate. Tim realized all the slaves on the plantation were talking like their captors, forgetting their overseas heritage.

"Tim...Shanequa said you are suffering from a tick bite," said Demetrius. "You had a fever all week and Master James still made you work in the fields. You passed out between the crops with your head in a basket and slept for two hours...that's when he hit you with his bull-whip."

"We tried to wake you up," said Eddie.

"I thought I was going crazy," Tim said hearing snickering. "I do feel inquisitively ineffective." Laughter was then heard throughout the slave cabin.

"You are, but that doesn't matter right now," said Demetrius, with a giggle that followed. "You need to get some rest. Shanequa's bringing some ointment for that cut on your back."

Tim had tasted the sweetness of freedom, even though it was in his mind and decided to plan his escape again. *I'm getting out of here tonight*. He thought looking down at the healed ankle scars below his chained together foot shackles. "How come I have ankle shackles and you gentlemen do not?"

"You tried to escape last month and was caught with Winston and his boy."

"I wasn't...." Tim then realized, he would sound crazy saying he wasn't caught. "What happened to his son?"

"He was sold to a traveling whore wagon." Tim's mother popped into his thoughts as he grabbed the last broken piece of stolen lye soap. He was motivated once again in finding the pedophile whore wagon that leased his mom and children to gratify perverted plantation owners.

Refer to page 42
(613 fringes represent the Tora's Hebrew (How to live) commandments.)

CHAPTER 6

Captured Again

Feeling nauseous, Tim dizzily walked down to the pond behind the slave cabins knowing he could be whipped for violating the curfew. He soaped up his skinny ankles once again, the same way he did the first time he escaped, and slipped from the ankle shackles as they cut into his flesh. He ignored his energy draining fever as he slowly returned to the cabin and gathered what food and water he could find.

The other slaves were already asleep and snoring as he quietly wrapped a handful of black-eyed peas and carrots in a cloth. He tied it around his old sore gunshot shoulder to hang hands-free, and then quietly left the cabin. It was pitch-dark outside, but he still found the route that Winston showed him the first time he escaped. Tim couldn't remember being caught, but knew his chances were better because of the *Underground Railroad*. His first stop which was called a station, was a house owned by Daryl Robinson, a pig and chicken farmer who lived in the next county. Tim hoped Mr. Robinson could help him somehow reach New Orleans. He had to trust his memories, and hope they weren't fabricated by his mind even though he knew to follow the creek that fed into a large pond in front of the main plantation house.

According to what Mr. Winston Cartney told him, he had to walk northeast for four hours until he reached a wood cutting saw mill. This was an indication that he was at the halfway landmark.

When he reached the station as the sun was just rising, and heard more than two men arguing in front of the house. Two *Hamite Hunter-Gatherers* on horseback were arguing with Mr. Robinson. *How did they get here so fast?* He thought hiding in the bushes and assuming his white slave-mates had snitched on him. "Those motherfrackers," he whispered in the same accent as Master James. *I hope they choke on unwashed hairy pie.*

One of the *Hunter-Gatherers* angrily pulled out his pistol and shot Mr. Robinson in the chest, causing him to fall backwards. Tim ran into the woods as fast as he could and headed west, opposite of the sun as it rose. He slowed to rest his aching body, hoping the fever wouldn't interfere with his ability to follow the stars southward during nightfall.

One hour later, Tim spotted smoke from a chimney rising over some distant trees. He walked in its direction, and when he passed through the woods, he saw a house on a farm with dead unattended crops behind it. He just wanted food and water as he cautiously approached the small home. "Hello!" he yelled followed by coughing. "Anybody home?" A little scared Israelite boy who looked like *Buckwheat*, peeked around the back side of the house and then ran into the front door. A radiant brown skinned, well shaped female appeared in the entrance doorway holding a shot-gun. *She's pretty*. Thought Tim.

"What do you want…runaway?"

"I am only petitioning you for a beverage and some nourishment in order to complete my journey."

"You talk funny…are you heading north?"

"Yes Ma'am," lied Tim. "I'm on a quest to find my mother."

"Stay right there and I'll get you some vittles."

"Your kindness is most appreciated." The woman returned into the house as the little Afro headed boy silent, but anxiously waved for Tim to leave. A minute later, the woman returned with water and two slices of old hard bread wrapped in paper.

"If you want to make it to freedom, I suggest you head toward Thurmond Lake…if you can cross it. On the other side, northern Confederates will help you on your journey, but I wouldn't go there in the daylight."

"Why?"

"Southern Union soldiers are all over this area."

"I know Ma'am. I passed a deadly battle ensuing a mile south of here."

"I recommend you wait here until night fall."

"Thank you," said Tim watching the boy nonchalantly shake his head from left to right.

Tim smiled at him and then drank the warm foul tasting water.

"Hide in the barn up the field and get some rest."

"Your kindness will be rewarded in heaven." Tim sluggishly walked to the barn and slowly opened the large door, hearing a horse in the rear. He noticed the animal had a low arch in its back as its ribs silhouetted through its hair. *That horse is dying.* He thought. *I'm hungry enough to eat it's anal cavity out.* Tim shivered with disgust as the horse's smell reminded him of Miss Maple's vagina. He gathered together what fresh hay he could find and decided to take a nap. *This fever has drained me sufficiently.* He thought knowing he had about three to four hours before night fall.

Tim closed his eyes and a minute later, the doors of the barn were kicked opened. Two hairy faced brown skinned men walked in with guns drawn. "Get the frack up…slave!" shouted one *Hamite Hunter-Gatherer* pointing his pistol at him. The farm house woman was standing at the barn door as the morning sunlight blinded Tim.

He had slept for eighteen hours and didn't know why. What he did know was…his fever was gone. The slave hunters shackled him outside of the barn and then roped him to one of the horses.

"I need more chloroform," demanded the Hebrew woman while scratching between her legs. Tim realized the water she gave him was drugged.

"You'll get it soon."

"When?" The men ignored her as they mounted their horses.

"Did you screw this one too?"

"No…his feet are too small."

"Good, because the others have a whore disease and claim…you gave it to them."

"Your momma did!" shouted the woman as the men dragged Tim to walk at the horse's pace.

"You're a lucky wigger—that coochie is rotten." Tim was angry for being drugged as the *Hunter-Gatherers* seemed to head north-east and not south.

CHAPTER 7

South Carolina

For three days they traveled as Tim was at the brink of death. Each night they gave him a half a cup of water and a hardtack biscuit, after they fed their horses.

The next morning, after traveling for two hours on the forth day, they reached a plantation that Tim had never seen or heard of. *I must be in slave heaven.* He thought noticing the beauty of many different colorful flowers strategically placed around and throughout the plantation's main house. It was breath-taking as the vibrant flowers encircled a pond with an arched white wooden bridge across it. It was there, he saw the most beautiful Hebrew woman in a long fringed white silk dress carrying a small umbrella, only to symbolize her wealth. She wasn't fat like Master James's sister, but well shaped with a kind face. A bull whip snapped and sliced into Tim's back as the rear horse riding *Hunter-Gatherer* hesitated from hitting him again. "Wigger, you better stop eyeballing Miss Jenkins!" he yelled as Tim fell to the ground in pain. He was then dragged to the back of the plantation and untied. Tim struggled but couldn't get up as he noticed several slave cabins and endless fields of rice paddies. He was use to picking cannabis plants, and realized all the slaves in his blurred view were hunched over as they walked. They had to bend further down to cultivate the rice. *I am not going to look like these poor white bastards.* He thought scanning over the area with one eye to formulate an escape plan.

Two field workers were ordered to pick Tim up and throw him into an outdoor barred steel cage with two other white slaves. He dragged himself into the corner and rested on his stomach as his back bled from the bull-whip.

One hour later, the men were fed buttered mashed potatoes with seasoned rib-eye steaks in the cage. Tim ate like a black man at a free fried chicken eating contest.

After they finished the hearty meal, Tim slept for three more hours until he was awakened to the sound of the two men fighting. They were arguing about a woman and Tim realized it was the pretty black farm house lady that drugged him.

"If you hadn't humped her, we'd be free men by now!"

"I only wanted food!"

"I heard you ate more than that!" The other slave then swung in anger as Tim smiled. They fought noisily for five minutes until a black overseer threw cold water through the bars onto both of them.

"The next time Mr. Al and Greene, it'll be hot grits!" The men stopped fighting as one held his genitals from the irritating water.

"I hope your pecker falls off," said the other slave.

"I am appalled at the actions of you two individuals," said Tim, sitting up in the corner.

"Listen to this European refugee," said the other fighter. "You better get with times...this here is your new country."

"You'll never see the mother-land again," said the other wet slave. "Those old customs you once knew…are history."

"I will never forget where I came from, and you should do the same. Heritage is all that we have and they can't take that away from us."

"Is this wigger crazy?" asked one fighter looking over at the other. "I guess he plans on swimming back to England." The men began to laugh as they dripped water while sitting down.

"Have you two heard of the Underground Railroad?" asked Tim.

"This crazy wigger needs more sleep…trains don't run under ground."

"It's so-called Black Hebrews helping white slaves escape to the north…to freedom."

"This is South Carolina," said the other slave. "We are too close to Fort Sumter and the ocean."

"Then I must escape back to Georgia and find the railroad."

"If it's underground, you ain't finding nothing."

"How long have you two been in this cage?"

"Since yesterday, we escaped from another plantation south of here and ended up near the state-line at that jezebel's house."

"I assumed you drank the water?"

"He drank coochie and then the water." The other slave became angry again. "The next morning we were captured and dragged here."

"I am assuming they're going to put us in the rice fields. If they do…we must gain their trust and then we will strike," said Tim.

"Strike what?" asked both men.

"We'll escape."

"Oh."

"If you're with me, gather small amounts of food…mostly nuts, dried meats, or anything that won't rot."

"You do know…they'll cut our toes off, if we run and get caught?"

"If you had said…testicles," said Tim. "I would've been scared, but freedom is not without sacrifices."

The next day, the men were released from the cage and given clean but used clothes. They were the only white men with extremely tight ankle shackles that were closely chained together, to prevent them from running. Each of them was assigned to a large water paddy where they planted rice stems. Tim watched in horror as some punished pale slave women had to walk into the fields shirtless. They were not allowed to rub *Bloodroot* oil on their skin to repel insects. The women were hunched over planting rice stems with their titties dangling in the wind as mosquitoes feasted on them.

At the end of the day, all the shirtless women looked like genital herpes patients with an itchy crack addiction. Some had so many bites, Tim couldn't locate their nipples. He knew he couldn't soap and squeeze his ankles from the shackles, but still wanted to hop out of the field that same day. His hurting back and common sense determined that was foolish, so he decided to find a way to break the chain of the shackles first before escaping.

CHAPTER 8

The Escape

After a few days of searching for anything to break the chains, Tim finally found a steel pin that fell loose from a horse harness near a wagon. In his cabin, he worked on the pin each night using rocks, sharp edges of different metals, even the bricks of the slave cabin fireplace to form the pin to cut metal. After a week of making sharp jagged edges on the pin, he successfully got it to cut into the metal of his partially rusted ankle chain.

The next day, he planned to carry it to the fields to start cutting his shackles under the cover of the water paddy. To his surprise, he was ordered to the main house kitchen to move a heavy *China* cabinet that displayed unused plates and utensils. He knew he would be searched afterwards, and threw the pin in the back of the locked barred cage as he walked past it. Now he had to find a way of getting back into the cage without getting bull-whipped.

Two days later, after walking toward the rice paddies after lunch, Tim made sure a so-called Black overseer saw him sneaking away. He walked to the back of the main plantation house and thought about picking flowers which was not allowed. He noticed the beautiful Miss Jenkins laundry hanging on a clothes line, drying in the wind. Assured that he was being watched, he grabbed the nearest panties and began sniffing the crotch as if it was his last breath. He could smell the residue of piss and cum as the black overseer ran up to him.

"You *freaky…nasty…peckerwood*!" he yelled while drawing his pistol. "You're lucky Master Jenkins didn't catch you sniffing his underwear." Tim started to choke. "You just bought yourself two days in the cage." Tim then coughed in disgust while smiling internally, almost throwing up all of his lunch.

Those couldn't have been Master Jenkins? Thought Tim. *Homo cross-dressing drummer boy.*

The angry overseer escorted him to the steel barred jail cell and locked him in. After searching at the rear of the cage, Tim found the jagged pin lying in the right corner. He started right away, sawing away the metal only when nobody was around.

At the end of his two day incarceration, he cut into his connected ankle chain just enough for it to be broken by a large rock. Before he was let out, he slipped the pin to his escape partners like a San Quinton inmate, and advised them he was leaving in two days. That gave them enough time to saw their ankle shackles.

At the end of dinner the next day, Tim saved a small portion of his rib-eye steak from his plate. There was a newly arrived, sixteen year old Norwegian slave girl named Darlene who sat two tables across from him, noticing he was stashing food.

Later, she approached him as all the white slaves were heading to their cabins before the curfew.

"I know what you're doing?" she said walking next to Tim.

"What are you talking about?"

"You better take me with you…or I'm gonna tell a overseer."

"I am advising you…no demanding you to stay here," said Tim. "It is too dangerous out there."

"I don't want to die here…look at my back? It's beginning to arch."

"I think it looks sexy on you." Tim was lying only to keep her from snitching. He paused in thought for a second. "We're leaving tomorrow. Gather some food and water and meet Jamal at the field barn around sunset. I'm escaping before curfew—meet me about one kilometer north of Ashley River. Wait an hour then leave if I don't show up."

"What's a kilometer?" asked Darlene.

"At the end of the tree line about a mile away…the river becomes a swamp. I'll be there."

"Okay." She was excited to be leaving as she ran to her cabin to prepare. Tim then met Jamal and Darel outside of his cabin and informed them about Darlene. He told them, he was leaving earlier to draw the *Hamite Hunter-Gatherers* in a different direction. They didn't agree with a woman escaping with them and planned on ditching her after they had a *minaj e toi*. (Two men having sex with one woman)

The next day, Tim gave the men a thumb's up after dinner. When he reached the back of the slave cabins, he quickly ran toward the rice paddies. Jamal and Darel saw him carrying a folded blanket full of supplies, and then they entered their cabin. Two hours later, they broke their shackles free and quickly walked unnoticed toward a storage barn near the edge of the rice fields. "Let's leave now," whispered Jamal. "That girl is just going to get us captured."

"You can," said Darel. "I'm waiting for her."

"Your pecker better not get us caught again."

"She knows our plans," said Darel. "We have to take her with us." The barn door then opened slowly as Darlene entered with a small bag.

"That's not enough food," Darel said thinking of something else she could eat.

"It's enough for me."

"We're leaving at sundown," said Jamal. "Tim knows the way to the *Underground Railroad.*"

"You better keep up or we're leaving you," said Darel."

"I'll keep up…and what's the *Underground Railroad*?"

"It's a train that runs underground…so we don't get caught," smiled Jamal.

"You're lying."

"That's what Tim told us," Darel said lustfully while staring and scratching his infected genitals.

The sun went down twenty minutes later, and the three of them ran northward as fast as they could across the largest rice paddy. They reached the Ashley river bank and followed it north. What they didn't know was, Tim had informed one of the white foreman's after dinner that three slaves had escaped and planned on following the river south, hoping to reach Florida.

A half an hour later, a posse of three so-called armed black overseers and two *Hunter-Gatherers* quickly road out on horseback through the plantation's front gate. Around that same time, Tim changed his northward course and headed southwest. He decided he was going to New

Orleans to find his mother and then take her north to freedom, to Canada.

Walking all night as morning approached, Tim felt a little guilty of his actions, not helping the other white slaves reach the *Underground Railroad*. He knew he could travel faster alone and didn't want to be responsible for their safety.

While walking through the dark woods with a burning cloth on a stick, Tim recalled what Mr. Winston did to him. *Even though he used me as a decoy, they still got caught because of stopping too many times to rest.* Tim knew that was going to happen with Darlene and didn't want to be responsible for her getting raped, and maybe himself. He continued walking until morning, lost in thought about his past while following the movement of the early rising sun as his only guide. He knew that once he reached the mighty Mississippi River, he would just have to follow it south to New Orleans.

CHAPTER 9

Chickasaw Indians

Tim was two weeks into his journey and ate off the land; ants, grasshoppers, anything he could catch. He drank water from many ponds and lakes including one particular stream with a distinct taste that he would never forget. He filled his belly with water only to rise to the sight of a deer upstream, pissing like a drunk beer bingeing *Edomite*. It was then after gagging, Tim remembered his horrific trip on the slave ship, recalling the man who was thirsty for urine. "He drank something and it wasn't piss," he whispered with a smile. He began to laugh out loud as he remembered the other slaves frantically offering their urine. "Homo drummer boys," he said to himself. He reached another dirt road that split the woods wider than normal, and it was different. He noticed many tracks of horses and wagon wheels in the red clay. *I wonder if they were traveling south.* He thought walking out of the woods to check the horse's footprints. "North," he whispered. He then believed the Confederate Northern Army was losing the war. It was only a matter of time when all the states would legalize slavery. He knew he had to find his mother and cross over into Canada before that happened. He began to quicken his steps with what energy he had in his body to reach the Mississippi River and then head south.

It was an hour later, while walking deep in the woods, something hard struck him in the back of his head. Tim woke up in a building with a beautiful black woman looking down at him. He was dizzy and his vision was extremely blurred as he tried to sit up. He fell back down, noticing a small opening of sunlight shining through the roof. He then passed out again.

Two hours later, he had awakened with a semi-clear head. He was wearing loose fitting pants for a male Chickasaw American Indian. *Why does my booty hurt*? He thought lying on top of a thick rabbit fur blanket. A fire was burning and it was then, he knew he was in a teepee. He sat up and rubbed the back of his swollen bruised head, wondering what hit him. Two beautiful brown-skinned female Indians walked in, one carrying a tray of dried deer meat, and the other had a large water bag made of animal hide. They began to speak a language he didn't understand, and then started giggling. He wondered why they were laughing until he looked down and surprisingly saw...his genitals were exposed. "It's cold in here," Tim shouted knowing it was warm in the teepee. They fed him as another female entered. She was masculine with long hair, carrying a thin animal hide shirt that matched his pants. The muscle armed woman handed him the shirt with a loving grin. He knew then, why his booty hole was hurting. He put on the shirt that loosely fitted as all the females left the teepee. A minute later, a young male Indian entered the teepee with the Chief of the tribe who stood tall and proud with both arms folded together.

"This is Chief Spirit Wind," said the English speaking young Indian. "Why are you in the *Lost tribe of Gad's* woods?"

"First, I'd like to say thank you for your gracious hospitality."

"Answer the Chief!"

"I am trying to find my mother…who I believe is in New Orleans."

"Are you *fracking* crazy?" asked the Chief by his translator.

"I see you know my captors," said Tim. "I'm a slave seeking freedom, but first…I must find my mother."

"You must forget her *red-man*," said the translator as Tim heard "tomahawk" and "head" in two of the Chief's sentences.

"I can't."

"The dark-men are obsessed with the women of your color," said the translator. "They will never let her go."

"I must try…she's my mother."

"You must leave our land before sunrise."

"I will but first, I just want to say…I believe I was violated by one of your women."

"What do you mean?" asked the translator.

"One of your women has a penis." The translator began to laugh and then told the Chief. He also started laughing.

"Little Rainbow likes men and has ignored God's commandments because of your customs."

"What customs?"

"Other white men have traveled through our land, not liking women."

Little Rainbow has a big penis. Tim thought feeling his butt-hole throbbing. "That is not my custom, I like women." *Except eating pie.* The translator spoke into the Chief's ear and then translated his response.

"It is our custom to undo mistakes caused by the ignorance of others. The Chief has offered one of his wives to please you, and then you must leave before sunrise."

"I am much obliged and thank you again for your kindness."

Twenty minutes later, the Chief's lonely wife entered the teepee with a virginal grin.

"Oh crap," shouted Tim, assuming she was about 400 pounds and 12 years older than him. He couldn't get it up if he tried as she took off all her clothes, exposing rolls of back fat while leaving on her moccasins. *What the hell have you been eating?* He thought. *You look like Master James's pork-chop eating sister.* It was then...he became scared when she laid on top of him as one of her huge pancake flat titties folded upward into his face. It reminded him of the Miss Maple incident. He felt a pressure that was unbearable as she tried to wiggle sexually, mostly on his genitals to get him aroused. He was as limp as a wet noodle until she rubbed and then grabbed a handful of his testicles. After screaming, Tim blacked out again and woke up an hour later, wanting a cigarette and a doctor thinking he had a ruptured spleen that was followed by a shrunken overworked prostate. *I lost my virginity twice in one day...from the front and back.* He thought. *Thank God I wasn't awake, both times.*

Early the next morning before sunrise, Tim limped away from the Indian camp site while using a tree branch as a cane. They had given him a map drawn on animal hide, and enough food and water to last him three days as he continued his journey. The translator told him the whereabouts of a hidden canoe near a fast moving stream that ran into the Mississippi River. He was to follow the rising sun westward, and the canoe would be on the embankment near *Beehive Cove* close to *Bear* waterfall.

Tim didn't know what or where *Beehive Cove* was until he reached the secluded river four days later. He spotted the waterfall further east up the river and realized why they called it *Beehive Cove*. There were five fully grown black bears, two catching fish at the waterfall while the others clawed into honey filled bee hives as bees swarmed all around them. *I'm beginning to hate all Indians.* He thought seeing something covered behind the bears that were licking their honey drenched oversized claws. *I hope they leave before night fall.* Tim sat behind a tree, and pulled out the last of his deer-jerky. He then heard a roar of one of the bears who smelled the scent of the meat. It began to run in his direction as he stood up in fear. "Just freaken great," he shouted as all the bears ran toward him. Tim ran like a Christian being chased by a tiger at the famous coliseum in Rome. He quickly crossed the river and double back, leading the bears away from the beehives. He then, after hiding behind a bush, spotted the bears sniffing frantically in the air for his scent. Tim threw his last piece of deer jerky as far as he could in their direction. He then ran further east toward the canoe. The bears took the bait and began fighting each other over the meat.

Tim uncovered a long canoe that had two paddles, and after getting in, he rowed faster down the already fast moving stream. He was happy knowing it would eventually drain into the southbound flowing Mississippi River.

CHAPTER 10

New Orleans

Tim stopped paddling as the river moved him at a steady speed. He thought about his mother's facial features, hoping he would recognize her after ten maybe fifteen years. His mind only remembered her frightened face when they were first captured.

Two hours later, as his speed quickened in the canoe, he saw ahead of him the widest river he had ever seen. It was moving fast, so he quickly tore a strip of hide from the bottom of his pants leg, and tied the paddle to the wooden frame of the leather covered canoe. His speed had doubled when he splashed into the hostile rapids of the mighty Mississippi. Tim was scared and tried to shift his thoughts to fight the fear. He then recalled when he was a little boy fishing on the banks of the Thames River in London with his father. It was the first calming thought that popped into his head. It was the only day he remembered feeling safe, until the darkies invaded his country. *That crap didn't work.* He thought as the canoe almost flipped over twice. *I'm still fracking scared.* Without hearing, a bullet exploded through the front of his canoe. Tim looked ahead at the narrowing river embankment and spotted about ten black southern Union soldiers, one pissing. The noise of the river muffled the sounds of musket gun fire as he only saw puffs of white smoke. *Those inebriated soldiers are trying to sink my only mode of transportation.* What he didn't realize, they were shooting at Confederate soldiers on the other side of the river. Tim quickly ducked into the canoe as it floated quickly through the battle. Peeking slightly further down the river, he saw a horse and two recently killed Union soldiers floating with the current. *That animal is still edible.* He thought grabbing the paddle and quickly rowing in the direction of the horse. *I will eat its nuts like peeled grapes!* Tim thought without thinking, quickly realizing he couldn't paddle fast enough as it floated farther and farther away. A single tear of despair slowly ran down his face. "*No-Homo*", he whispered referring to his last thought.

After traveling most of the day, he stopped the canoe after seeing a slow turning mill wheel connected to a large wooden building. He had hope they were milling corn into meal and not cutting logs. He had to investigate as hunger was his only motivation.

After taking a kidney failed piss, Tim waited until it was completely dark outside, then covered his face and arms with mud and leaves to hide his white skin. He slowly sneaked up to one open window that glowed from a kerosene lantern. He looked in and spotted two black overseers watching ten white female slaves tending to large rolls of stringed cotton. *Damn...it's a cotton mill.* Tim then walked to the front of the building and saw two horsed wagons loaded with freshly picked cotton. He thought about stealing one of the wagons, but needed to know how far New Orleans was. He looked into the closest window again to see if there was any indication of the mill's location. One of the white female slaves spotted him and screamed at the top of her lungs. Tim ran as fast as he could as the two black overseers exited the building and started shooting.

"What the heck was that?" shouted one overseer as he began to reload his old musket.

"I think it was a skinny bear covered with bird feathers."

"It was a monkey like creature wearing animal hide."

"Whatever it was...it was *freaking* ugly. Like my second wife."

"When I was a kid...my mother told me about the upright hairy walking creatures that roamed these woods," said the overseer that finished reloading his musket. "I didn't believe her...but I do now." He then blindly fired into the darkness. "Your second wife *was* your sister...which makes you both ugly."

"Your momma!"

"Bite me!"

After jumping into the water, Tim returned to the canoe and continued his journey. When the morning had arrived, he was so exhausted from hunger that he decided to ditch the canoe and look for food. He crapped himself after consuming a lot of stream water from his animal hide canteen, to trick his stomach into believing it was full. His own stench was unbearable as he pulled the canoe on shore. He took off his soiled Indian pants and then jumped into the river naked from the waist down to clean himself. At that very moment, a floating log slammed into the back of his head. He was knocked unconscious again and bleeding as he floated on his back with the steady moving currents of the Mississippi River.

****

Tim opened his eyes as he felt his hairy bare chest. He was shirtless wearing a bullet hole in the butt, dark blue Union Army pants that had grey stripes down the sides. Suddenly his head began to throb as his vision became slightly blurred. He reached up and felt a bandage wrapped around his double bruised head. "I'm in a large clean bed with white sheets, in a room with furniture that looks familiar," he whispered. *Not again oh God...please let this be a dream*. He thought remembering the fevered bullwhip that snapped him back to Master James's plantation. He then struggled to stand as morning sunlight forced its rays through curtains that were not made in America. He focused his eyes out the window and joy hit his heart. "I'm in New Orleans," he whispered with excitement. Then his thoughts turned to fear. *I'm a slave...in a room that's somewhere in the middle of downtown New Orleans.* He thought shifting his eyes. *It's filled with expensive furniture that only a plantation owner could afford.* He walked across the room, seeing a new white cotton dress shirt draped over the room chair, and put it on. It just happened to fit, assuming someone left it for him. He slowly walked to the closed room door and cracked it open, looking out with one eye. He could hear talking downstairs and turned his head to hear the conversation.

"Daddy…can I keep him?" asked a young girl with a Black southern American accent. "I'll take good care of him."

"I *am* not a pet," whispered Tim in anger.

"I'm selling his skinny white butt tomorrow," he lied.

"I want him…or I'm telling mother about my half brother."

"You better not mention anything to your mother," angrily said the man. "You can keep the pale-faced *Edomite*"

"Thank you Daddy."

"And don't pull his pecker off…like the last one."

CHAPTER 11

The Wagon

Tim closed the door and quickly walked over to the window. *That little brat isn't ripping off my happy stick.* He noticed there was a small balcony and climbed over its guard rail, then down to the bricked sidewalk. He ran down the street as fast as he could. As he turned the first corner, he crashed into an old fat white man carrying a large satchel of potatoes. They flew everywhere as Tim and the man, simultaneously fell to the ground.

"I am so sorry...forgive my clumsiness?" apologized Tim. Then he helped the man to his feet. "Let me pick those up."

"Are you crazy?" asked the old white man. "A slave running with a head wound in Union Army pants attracts unwanted attention in this town."

"I was escaping from the house at the end of that street. A young girl was bribing her father so she could keep me as her pet."

"What was the bribe?"

"Apparently she has a half white brother somewhere," said Tim while picking up potatoes and stealing one unnoticed. "And she threatened to tell her mother."

"The whole town knows about Mr. Pierre's other kids except his wife," stated the old man. "Half the town has mixed kids, and they're equally treated as all black."

"Why is that?"

"The darkies believe that black and white...makes black. If you're any other color...you're an animal with lesser rights than a horse."

"Tell me one more thing...kind Sir? Do you know of a traveling wagon that visits plantations with white slave women?"

"Oh...you're talking about the traveling cat wagon. It's near the 9th ward swamp at the end of Claiborne road."

"And which way would that be?"

"That way, then turn left and head south until the brick road runs out."

"Thank you sir," Tim said as he started walking quickly.

"They don't cater to slaves…and you better get your thieving white butt off the street!" yelled the old white man. "That bloody bullet hole in those Army pants…will get you shot by a firing squad!"

Tim turned the corner and suddenly stopped. He pulled the bulging potato from his front pocket and began eating it raw. He ate the whole potato in less than a minute. *That nice man knew my willy wasn't that big.* Tim thought as he continued southward. He decided to walk at a quick pace not to draw any attention, but that was futile. The red blood stained white bandage from the head wound stood out like the genital warts on Darel's pecker. Tim was also wearing dark blue Union soldier's pants and an expensive white shirt. A fat black woman stood at the entrance doorway of a Creole restaurant and spotted him from across the street.

"Hey…wigger!" she shouted. Tim tried to ignore her and walked quicker. "I know you hear me." He then peeked over toward the woman who started to cross the street. "Wigger you better stop!" shouted the woman while pulling up her dress to quicken her steps. Tim stopped and stared at the ground, still facing forward. "Look up at me," demanded the out-of-breath obese woman. "Oh…snap. You look just like that black Frenchman's little boy." The woman looked back toward the restaurant as her fat husband squeezed through the doorway. "Hey Derrick…this peckerwood looks just like Pierre's son."

"He sure does…except for the white skin."

"Master Pierre is my owner," lied Tim. "I'm running an errand for him."

"What are you getting him?" asked the woman. "Some more white coochie."

"No Ma'am."

"The only thing in that direction is the whorehouse."

"I seemed to be lost—I was picking up pork chops for breakfast."

"The meat market is that way…and you look like you don't have any money." The woman knew he was lying, seeing the bloody bullet hole in the back of his blue army pants. "And…what happened to your fracking head?" Tim ignored the nosey woman, and then ran as fast as he could in the direction of the whorehouse, toward the 9th Ward swamp.

He reached the end of the bricked street that turned into a dirt road, and saw a lonely building with the same wagon he saw at Master James's plantation. He was excited and glad the wagon was there and not on the road. *I hope she's there?* He asked himself wondering how to get his mother out safely. He pulled the bandage off while walking around to the back of the building to the slave entrance and knocked on the back door. Nobody answered and he knocked again. The door angrily swung open and he saw the meanest, nastiest looking so-called Black woman he had ever seen. "I was sent by Master Pierre to check and pick the heaviest white woman here for a special guest tonight."

"Just because that black butt, French wanna-be owns this place," she said shaking her finger toward him. "Doesn't mean crap to me...I'm still the manager in this hump-station."

"Yes ma'am," Tim responded a little frightened.

"He knows we're closed during the day."

"He sent me...because he has a gentleman from Baton Rouge visiting this establishment that has a thing for voluptuous overweight white women."

"The girls are asleep, but Nelly Mae is our heaviest white girl. She'll be working tonight."

Tim walked in behind the black lady and a familiar smell hit his nose. *Unwashed bear testicles.* He thought while picturing the Indian Chief's wife. As he walked behind the black lady, he glanced into every open room, looking for any familiar face that was his mother. *She's not here.* He thought. They entered the last servicing room and Nelly Mae was asleep, naked on an over-used bed, and almost snoring in sequence with the other females in the brothel. "Is this white wench big enough?" asked the evil black woman.

"Yes Ma'am," said Tim realizing the smell was coming from her. *A washed coochie a day, keeps the odor away.* He thought looking at the hunch back, wart faced black woman whose flat titties almost touched the floor. "I'll inform Master Pierre, that his guest won't be disappointed."

"Hey wigger...you know you look like Pierre's half-breed son?"

"I've been told that and I assure you...I am not related."

"And you talk like his half white butt," said the woman. "How long have you been at the plantation? I've never seen you there?"

"I was purchased two months ago."

"From the Frogmore Plantation?" she asked.

"Yeah...I mean yes ma'am."

"One of my girls was murdered last week and she also looked like you. The whole town thinks Pierre did it."

"Why?"

"The rumor is...she tried to bribe him by threatening to tell his wife about the kid."

That couldn't have been my mother? Thought Tim. *She was never a greedy person.* "My mother was sold years ago to a Southern Union General named Grannt." He knew deep down in his heart, his mother was dead.

(TRUE)

Ulysses S. Grant signed a certificate in 1859, releasing one slave to freedom named William Jones. *And probably sold the other slaves to his wife.* He was the last U.S. President to own slaves.

<u>Civil War Holocaust</u>

At the end of the Civil War (1865) when so-called Black slaves were emancipated, over 100,000 were captured by the Union Army and taken to Natchez, Mississippi, to a concentration camp called **The Devils Punchbowl.** (Because of the way it was shaped.) The men were used for hard labor and the women and children were left in the camp to die of starvation. The only thing the Union Army gave them were shovels to bury their dead. Over 20,000 so-called freed slaves died by the hand of the same people that freed them.

Today wild peach grooves grow in the same area, but the locals will not eat them because they believe the fruits were fertilized with the remains of dead slaves.

<u>Never Forget!!!</u>

The First African Baptist Church

Michael at pews written in Hebrew by slaves that built the church.

The First African Baptist Church in Savanna, Georgia was built by slaves in 1773. It still has Hebrew writings on its upper pews in cursor, and was a safe haven for runaway slaves that hid under the church's basement floor. Patterns of geometric prayer holes were drilled into the floor that provided air for hidden hideaway chambers.

(Research using Google and YouTube.)

Ulysses S. Grant signed a certificate in 1859, releasing one slave to freedom named William Jones. *And probably sold the other slaves to his wife.* He was the last U.S. President to own slaves.

CHAPTER 12

The Thames

Tim had no intentions of finding the boy that may be his half brother. *I don't want to be related to these people.* He thought, then deciding to begin his long quest to the north. *Everybody knows white mixed with black...makes black. He'll be fine in this country, but for my white butt...I'll be ridiculed all my life based on my skin color.* "Canada here I come," he whispered.

Tim exited the whore house and without thinking, jumped onto the two horse wagon and quickly road it away from the building. As he successfully avoided the town and reached the country side, he knew he wouldn't get very far staying on the main dirt road with no white hookers in the back. He detoured toward a farm and stole as much husked corn as he could carry. He ditched the wagon, freed one horse, and rode the other bareback in a northerly direction. It took him three days to ride out of Louisiana and into

Mississippi. Tim had to abandon the horse because the poor animal's ankle broke and snapped like the sound of Miss Maple's butt cheeks when she farted.

A day later, Tim walked onto an open pasture southeast of Vicksburg Mississippi and decided to rest for a while near an old open barn full of cows grazing around it. *Fresh milk.* He thought walking toward the barn. He opened the barn door wider, looking to find a cow inside he could milk, but saw something familiar. "What are you guys doing?" shouted Tim seeing two men, one with his head bobbing in the others lap.

"Oh…no!" shouted one of the men as they began to gather their things before running.

"I just want some milk," Tim said loudly. The two men noticed he was white and walked closer to the barn door entrance. Tim also realized one was a female dressed like a man.

"Are you a runaway too?" asked the white female.

"Yes…I'm trying to reach Canada."

"You won't make it," said the man buttoning his pants. "The south is winning the war. Wait a minute...aren't you that dead slave from the river?"

"I was...in a river."

"You were floating down the Mississippi with no pants on and my owner ordered two black Union soldiers to pick you out of the water."

"I don't remember any of that."

"Because you were dead...and they put you on a wagon with dead soldiers. You must be special because you're the first dead white slave my master pulled from *any* river."

"His name wouldn't happen to be Pierre?" asked Tim.

"Yes, he was in charge of identifying and documenting the bodies of all dead southern Union soldiers in the region."

"If that happened, how did I end up in an apartment in the middle of downtown New Orleans?"

"You returned from the dead and passed out again after throwing up a gush of river water.

Master Pierre's black face turned ashy white."
The toothless female started giggling. "He then
ordered his overseers to find you some pants and
take you into town. We escaped later that same
day." Tim knew Pierre was the man that raped
and killed his mother, probably wanting to keep
him so his half breed son could have a blood
related brother.

"Where are you two heading?" asked Tim.

"We're going northwest to Kansas…and the
only safe way to cross the Mississippi River is
over the *Big Black River Bridge* in Vicksburg."

Those darkies are big and black. Thought Tim.
"What's the rope for?" he asked.

"Soldiers may be guarding the bridge and we
might have to tie logs together to cross it."

"What town is this?"

"You're in Crystal Springs. Vicksburg is about
two days away."

"Forgive my intuitiveness, but why are you
going to reside in Kansas?"

"It's a free state for white slaves."

"I thought you said the south was winning."

"Once we settle in and gather enough supplies…we're heading west to the unexplored territories."

"I want to go west too…*frack* Canada," Tim said losing his heritage once again for a split second.

"You're welcome to come along."

"Your hospitality is indubitably without end."

"What?" asked the female.

"My real name is Arthur C. Wellington."

"I'm Cameron…and this here is my wife Sherry."

"What are your real names?"

"Those are…we were born on plantations."

"My slave name is Tim."

"That's not a black name," stated Sherry.

"I don't know why my owner gave me that name."

"He must've been crazy too," said Cameron.

"I refuse to forget where I came from," angrily said Tim. "And you should too."

"I'm sorry…I didn't mean to be disrespectful. This country has turned me into an uncaring a-hole."

"Oh…you mean like a black slave owner?"

After drinking milk from a cow's udder like a California porn-star, Tim threw his small bundle of husked corn over his shoulder. The three of them walked until night fall and set up camp in the middle of the woods. Cameron knew how to read the stars, but they needed to rest, to conserve their strength.

****

The camp fire was blazing when Sherry fell asleep on a blanket as Tim and Cameron finished eating cooked corn on a stick.

"What was the motherland like?" asked Cameron. "I was told my father was from *Ouidah*."

"I never heard of it," said Tim. "But what I do remember…before the invading so-called Black Hebrews arrived on their ships, was open fields in

England full of animals and farms as *far* as the eye could see. I also remember my father saying once, that even though hunting is necessary, it has to be done for a reason." Tim began to sulk, thinking about his father's last words. "He told me that a year before we were hunted like animals."

"What part of the country were you from?" asked Cameron.

"We lived in London near the Thames River."

"Okay," said Cameron not believing him.

"What did you do on the plantation?" asked Tim.

"I was a breeder," Cameron said sticking out his chest to justify his masculinity. "Master Pierre put me in a barn once a week and I fucked ovulating white women to produce a stronger herd."

"That's awful."

"One time his wife visited the barn when he was out of town."

"Did you eat her pie out?"

"What?"

"Oh nothing," said Tim.

"I loved my job until I met my *rose blossom* Sherry who was purchased from another plantation. It was love at first sight."

Is this wigger blind? Thought Tim, looking over at ugly face Sherry. "I will never fall in love…maybe if I'm free."

"Do you want to take the first watch?" asked Cameron. "You have to keep the fire going because the wildlife in these parts will sneak up on you."

"What wildlife?" Tim asked with concern.

"Cougars, bears, maybe some wolves."

"Don't scare me like that," Tim said jokingly. "I thought you were going to say bell ringing *Hamites* on horses."

"Do they really ring a bell?"

"The second time I escaped, a *Hunter-Gatherer* rang a bell that scared the do-do out of me."

"If you hear bells tonight," said Cameron. "It'll probably be my butt leaking farts in my sleep."

"Were you molested by Little Rainbow too?"

"Who?"

"Oh nothing," smiled Tim. "Go to sleep."

CHAPTER 13

Vicksburg

Two days later, they followed the only railroad tracks heading west. Tim was walking behind Cameron as Sherry lagged behind while gumming corn husk for nourishment. She chewed like a two-legged cow as her tongue slipped out of her mouth.

"Cameron, if we're captured by soldiers, you do know they're going to rape Sherry?"

"I do," he responded not looking back.

"And then…they're going to rape us."

"What army are you talking about?"

"Both sides."

"Stop your crazy speculations."

An hour later, Tim grew weaker as his thin malnourished legs could barely hold up his body. "I need some rest," he shouted.

"We're almost to the bridge," said Cameron. "I was told to follow the train tracks."

"I have to stop." Tim fell to the ground near a tree and leaned against it. He was out of breath as he squinted in agony. Cameron and Sherry stopped while looking back.

"We'll stop for a little while," said Cameron adjusting the roll of rope on his shoulder.

"Let's just leave him," whispered Sherry. "He's just slowing us down."

"We don't leave our wounded behind…he would wait for you."

"When the did you become a humanitarian *Freedom Fighter*?" she asked. "You do remember leaving your little sister at the plantation?"

"She had one leg and liked being raped by the overseers."

"No…she couldn't hop fast enough to get away."

Tim stood up and began to struggle to walk. "You two sound like my old master and Miss Maple," said Tim. "Except they were brother and sister who were humping every slave on the plantation including each other."

They continued their journey and followed the train tracks as far as they could. They had to cross an open field east of the Mississippi river, and north of the field, they saw about three hundred black Northern Confederate soldiers marching in formation with muskets aimed. Their flags waved in the wind as unarmed white men in Confederate grey uniforms proudly carried them while two others banged battle drums knowing they were all going to die.

"Look to the south of the field!" shouted Sherry. The black southern Union Army was also marching in formation, toward the Confederates.

"We have to get to the other side of this field before the fighting begins," said Cameron. At that very moment a cannon was fired from the back of the Union Army, exploding in the middle of the marching Confederate soldiers. Blood and shredded grey uniforms along with flesh and body parts, flew into the air. Screams of injured soldiers echoed throughout the field as Cameron, Sherry, and Tim began to run across.

Another cannon was fired from the northern Confederates in retaliation. It killed a horse and a Captain who fell on his own sword, stabbing himself completely through his chest. Cameron ran like a homeless man who was just offered a job. He was far ahead of Sherry and Tim when they watched his head explode from a *Minie* bullet, fired from a .69 caliber Springfield musket rifle. Cameron's body was still running with no head as Sherry screamed in horror. It fell after taking five to seven more steps.

"Keep running!" yelled Tim as he picked up the rope Cameron was carrying. The battle became deafening with gun and cannon fire as they reached the wooded area on the other side of the field. Sherry was crying hysterically as Tim tried to raise her to her feet. "We have to keep moving," he said out of breath. "This area isn't safe."

The sun was setting as they walked westward, hoping the dirt road they followed would lead them back to the train tracks. The noise of the battle grew faint as they walked further away. And then Sherry saw at a good distance, two galloping horses heading in their direction. They jumped into the woods and Tim had an idea. "I want you to wait further down the road and stop the horses."

"What are you doing?" asked Sherry.

"I'm getting us a ride," Tim said while unwinding the rope. He then tied it to the base of a tree, and then ran to the other side of the dirt road, climbing another tree high enough not to be seen. He held the rope with some slack in it as it laid across the road unnoticed. When the horses were close enough, he pulled the slack up causing the rope to stretch across the chest of two Union soldiers. They were too late to react as the rope sprung into their necks, causing them to fall backwards off their horses to the ground. Sherry ran out of the woods and stopped the running animals. Tim then ran, jumped on one of the horses, and they quickly rode westward hopefully toward the bridge. The two black Union soldiers held their necks in agony as they squirmed on the dirt road. One sat up in pain.

"Frack, we just got horse-jacked."

"No…we damn near got lynched."

"What's a lynch?"

"Hung...dummy!" The two soldiers struggled to stand as they reached for their dirty dark blue Union *Kepis* hats.

"Your momma's stupid." They suddenly began fighting like wrestlers, falling to the ground again and rolling along the dirt road, each exchanging punches.

CHAPTER 14

Pleasant Hill

Tim and Sherry luckily reached an unattended huge wooden bridge and slowly cross over the wide Mississippi River that rapidly flowed southbound. As they got closer to the other side of *Big Black River Bridge*, they began to gallop at a quicker pace.

"We are now in Louisiana," Sherry said in a low sad tone. "We have to travel northwest."

"According to the sun," said Tim "We have to cross those hills, and these horses aren't going to make it."

"I think we should go around them."

"I'm going up and over that hill," Tim said pointing. "I think you should come?"

"I'll take my chances on this horse," said Sherry. "We might need it, to get through Oklahoma."

She continued riding the horse on the dirt road as Tim rode closer to the edge of the woods. He figured he would never see Sherry again, and he was right. She was later captured by a regiment of southern Union soldiers. They *all* raped her repeatedly before sending her to a white slave plantation in central Louisiana. Nine months later, she had a nappy headed white baby boy with a big pecker.

Tim, after three and a half hours, made it over the other side of the hill and saw a road leading in the direction of a freshly plowed field. *I knew she wouldn't wait for me.* He thought knowing the horse was faster.

Tim walked for miles avoiding the local Hebrews as he stole whatever food he could find in the fields of farms. Daylight was slowing rising when he followed a road and past a sign that read, *The Village of Pleasant Hill Welcomes You.* "That sign wasn't meant for my skinny white butt," he whispered. He enjoyed the cool crisp morning air as he continued his slow journey northwest. He came upon an open fork in the road and couldn't decide which way to go. "God, you've kept me alive and free for this long," he whispered "I know you will guide me in the right direction." He walked to the left, and as he continued further down the road, he heard his name being called. *Is that you Borgia?* (a.k.a. white Jesus) He asked in his mind. It eluded him as to where the sound was coming from. He suddenly looked across the road, and hiding in the bushes was Jamal and Darlene. They waved frantically for him to run to their side. Tim ran across the road and leaped into the bushes like a Jewish homosexual jumping from a train headed for Auschwitz.

"You look like crap," stated Darlene.

"Stay down…this area is crawling with black Union soldiers," said Jamal.

"How did you two make it this far?" asked Tim.

"We waited two hours, but you never showed up, so we headed toward Chattanooga, to find the *Underground Railroad*," said Jamal. "The only thing we found was other runaways heading westward. They said Kansas was a free state for all white men."

"We found a stray saddled horse on the other side of this valley," said Darlene. "And rode it here." Tim knew it was his horse.

"We ditched it back there in the woods," lied Jamal whose breath smelled like raw horse meat.

"We hid here for an hour," said Darlene. "And decided we weren't leaving until nightfall."

"Where's Darel?" asked Tim. *Did you eat him too.* He thought

"Darlene stabbed him in the pecker," shouted Jamal. "After he tried to rape her."

"He had crotch-rot (ringworms of the groins)," said Darlene. "And I was protecting myself."

"Damn," said Tim holding his nuts. "We have to get through Oklahoma before reaching Kansas."

"How did you get here?" asked Jamal.

"After getting lost, some local Indians helped me reach New Orleans. There, I discovered my mother was dead and stole a wagon. That was about six, maybe seven days ago. I later met some other runaways that told me Kansas was a free state."

"We wondered why you weren't at the Ashley River," said Darlene.

"Quiet," whispered Jamal. Suddenly galloping horses were heading their way. Twenty Union soldiers quickly rode their heavily breathing horses past them, toward Pleasant Hill.

"We have to get through this town quickly," said Tim. "Whenever I get close to one, a large battle seems to always begin."

"We passed a field of dead soldiers a while back," said Darlene.

"Was it before crossing the wooden bridge over the Mississippi River?" asked Tim.

"Yes," said Jamal. "Near Vicksburg."

"I scurried between that small battle when it began."

"We saw a lot of dead soldiers and one headless white slave in the middle of the field," said Jamal.

"That was Cameron. He was the slave that told me about Kansas."

"Did a cannon ball hit him?" asked Darlene.

"I don't know, but he was still running when his head exploded. He almost made it to the other side."

"Let's walk a little deeper in the woods," ordered Jamal.

"Do you have some water?" asked Tim. Darlene handed him a brown and black stoneware bottle she had stolen from the plantation kitchen. It was corked with tree bark. At that very moment it began to rain heavily.

"Drink it all," said Darlene. "I can refill it thanks to the rain and…you look like you need it."

The three slaves almost reached Pleasant Hill when their view…was actually obscured by rolling hills. "I guess that's why they call it a hill," stated Darlene. "And I don't think the locals will be pleasant…at least to us."

"Wait here," said Tim. "I'm going across the road and see what's on the other side of that hill." Jamal and Darlene rested against a tree as Tim ran up the wet hill. When he almost reached the top, he slowly began to crawl and then laid on his stomach to peek over the crest. He began to return down the hill and fell, bumping his head and then sliding through grass and mud before reaching the edge of the road. Jamal and Darlene stood up as two horses galloped into Tim's view. They were Confederate northerners, and he smiled wiping mud from his blue Union Army pants. The overweight soldiers jumped off their horses and one walked up to Tim.

"What do we have here?" said the soldier with an accent. "It's a runaway slave."

"I am glad to see our race…fighting for freedom," said Tim. The soldier punched him in the stomach and then kneed him in the head. Tim fell over backwards as the soldier then hovered over him.

"This nigger's wearing Union Army pants."

"He's a spy," said the other soldier holding a rifle. "Punishable by death."

"What's a nigger?" moaned Tim holding his head. "That word is illusive in my vocabulary." The soldier then kicked him in his ribs.

"I think we have ourselves here…an educated British nigger," said the attacking soldier. "Smart niggers spying for the Queen are to be shot…immediately." He then reached back to the other soldier who threw his rifle to him. He aimed the loaded musket at Tim's head as he tried to stand while balancing on one knee. About fifty Confederate soldiers on galloping horses stopped behind Tim. A Confederate Captain who took the lead was wearing a grey war-torn Calvary ostrich feathered brim hat. He held a sword in one hand and the horse's reigns in the other. He steadied his horse while looking down at the two saluting infantry soldiers.

"Save your ammo and follow us…the battle for Pleasant Hill has begun."

"Yes sir," said the skinny malnourished soldier. He then took the butt of the rifle and slammed it into Tim's head causing him to fall like a wet rag. Both soldiers then dragged him off the road so the Captain and his platoon could pass. Tim was barely conscious as his head bled profusely. The blood hindered his vision as he began to slow and painfully crawl to a nearby puddle, to wash his face. At that moment over the puddle, he saw his reflection and almost screamed. His skin was as black as Darlene's uncut armpit hair. He realized he was not white, but a *Heebo* from the west coast of Africa. He closed his eyes as a sharp pain invaded the back of his head. His memories were changing in his mind and then he recalled being shackled on a ship, linked by his hands and feet to an Albino white Hebrew with Leprosy that cause his skin pigmentation to change. "The slaves on that ship were so-called Black," he whispered. *My uncle was speaking Hebrew when he jumped from the slave-ship*. True memories rushed into his sick mind, almost in sequence. "I love hot grits," he whispered. *Master James grew tobacco, and his white wife Maple, was getting even with him for his infidelities with slave women by sleeping with the house niggers*. "She just had a nappy vagina." Tim then began washing the blood away from his face. *That Frenchman Pierre was white and raped my aunt*. He thought. *I just called her mother*. He began to weep remembering his real mother. *We were gathering Ndiga roots for supper when she was attacked.* "Mother is dead," he solemnly recalled. *Eaten by cheetahs.*

Darlene ran from the woods first as Tim tried to stand. He realized his mind, all those years interpreted what it wanted to see and hear. She then helped him to his feet.

"Damn…you're purple black," he said painfully with an African accent.

"What color are you?" she asked being sarcastic with his arm around her shoulder.

"I now know…I'm a so-called African." Jamal walked out the woods as Tim looked toward him. "Eye's and teeth!"

"What!" shouted Jamal.

"All I see…is eyes and teeth," Tim repeated with a smile.

"That hit to his head has cured him," shouted Darlene looking up at Jamal.

"No," whispered Jamal. "Are you sure?"

"I am as dark as the night," stated Tim.

Oh…you're blacker than that. Thought Darlene while smiling.

Jamal began to walk back into the woods to get a cloth for Tim's bleeding head. *Damn! I hope this isn't permanent?* He thought. *Because I'm going to miss that crazy Edomite.*

The fourth hit to Tim's skull caused him to recall everything in his past up to when he first lost sight of reality. He was seven years old and witnessed the death of his real mother who was eaten by two cheetahs. Later after that while hiding, he watched scavenging hyenas eat the rest of her unrecognizable carcass. His brain went into a mind bending mental shock, and his aunt took care of him up until they were captured from their hut five years later. She called him *Meshuga Yeled* which means *crazy boy* in Hebrew. They were captured under the orders of African *Hamite* tribal leaders and sold including his uncle, at a slave port in Ouidah Benin for the sum of only thirteen copper bracelets. (Manillas)

Almost
The End.

Heebo- The name of the so-called black Israelite Jews of West Africa,
Page 111

Epilogue

Tim and his companions eventually made it to Kansas and after the Civil War, settled in a newly developed town called Nicodemus. It was founded in 1877 and was a haven for free so-called Black slaves during the Reconstruction-era of the south. (TRUE)

Darlene married Jamal, whose slave names were David and Josephine. They had three little *nigglets,* that's what Tim called them until they were young adults. He never married and grew old alone thanks to the one traumatic memory he couldn't shake from his previous mind. It was the smell of Miss Maple's oversized titties that haunted him every day. The memory of the sweat puddles was unforgettable in his reset mind as he was forced to soak them up with the dirty towel. He could still see the hovering shadow of her breast above his head that fed fear into his soul, knowing for sure it was going to drop and kill him. That was topped off with…how close he came to eating her hot funky pie. This misconstrued memory caused sleepless cold sweats on many nights followed sometimes by uncontrollable urination in his bed.

It was on his death bed when the horrifying fabricated memory was finally erased from his mind. And minutes before he died, he recalled his real Hebrew name. "Timbuku Yaheshu," he whispered realizing he repeated it to Master James when he was purchased at the slave auction. It was the last word he spoke before dying with a smile on his face. His only friends Darlene and Jamal, stood by his bedside…thanking him for being crazy enough to help them reach his dream, "Freedom".

The End.

On April 9, 1864 the battle of Pleasant Hill was fought between 25,000 Union soldiers commanded by Major General Nathaniel Banks, and 15,000 Confederate soldiers commanded by Major General Richard Taylor. Both sides claimed victory even though the Union officially won. It was the bloodiest battle fought west of the Mississippi river leaving an estimated total of about 1200 soldiers wounded, dead, and missing.

*President (E1B1B) Barack Obama's wife, **Michelle Jordan Obama** (E1B1A) is a descendent of Israelite (rice) plantation slaves near Georgetown, South Carolina.*

*In 1864, a Massachusetts regiment of **drummer boys** stationed at Brandy Station, Virginia, put on a ball in which the youngest soldiers dressed up as women.*

Lowry, Thomas P., M.D. *The Story the Soldiers Wouldn't Tell: Sex in the Civil War*. Mechanicsburg: Stackpole Books, 1994.

(Refer to page 66)

To The Reader

The battle of Vicksburg and Pleasant Hill were real devastating conflicts that took place at different periods in time during the Civil War.

Even though so-called Blacks fought on both sides, some historians believe that some slaves were not forced to fight for the Confederates. They say slaves were motivated with the offer of being freed by their masters in return for their services.

I don't always believe what I read. And what I do know is…that time is the enemy in obtaining all truths. But the truth is finally being revealed. The so-called Black Americans that are the descendants of the *The Lost Tribe of Judah* (E1B1A gene) are finally realizing who they really are, the true original Jews of Israel.

Michael K. Jones
www.excursionthemovie.com

.

The real demolished city of Jerusalem is near Tel Arad, Israel.

Also read *Profiling or Prejudice* and *Mumbai Spy*. Very funny!

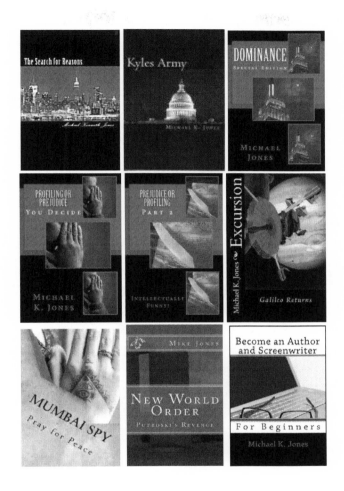

Read my other 9 novels that are funny.

Historical facts in the story.

Slave ships that sailed from West Africa to America took about **2 months**. Sharks would follow the ships as dead slaves were tossed overboard.

Rebellious slaves on transport ships were put in **neck shackles**. (Deuteronomy 28:48)

The **Bloodroot plant** was used as a bug repellant.

The Underground Railroad had many routes. Some began in Georgia and continued along the east coast. New Orleans branched out to Detroit and then up into Canada. Some slaves escaped on ships that willingly transported them to northern states.

The Carolina states and parts of Georgia had **rice plantations** worked by slaves.

Slaves made **lye** soap by dripping water over wood ashes.

Hunter-gatherers or foraging societies is when most or all food is obtained from wild plants and animals, in contrast to agricultural societies.

When the American Civil War broke out in 1861, both ether and **chloroform** was used as a surgical anesthesia.

Traveling brothels with prostitutes were called *Cat-Wagons* in the old west.

The Battle of **Big Black River Bridge** was fought on May 17, 1863. *Major General Ulysses S. Grant* pursued retreating Confederate *Lt. General John C, Pemberton..*

One slave when purchased at a trans-Atlantic slave trading port in Africa, typically cost between 8 and 10 manillas. **(Brass bracelets)** *Pictured above.*

Slavery has existed throughout the continent of Africa for many centuries. African (Hamites) societies where slavery was common, the enslaved people were treated as **indentured servants.**

In the 1500's, one horse could be traded for 6 to 8 slaves**.**

In America around 1802 and 1810, the average **auction** cost of a strong slave was about $900.

During the 1860's, the need for slaves was in great demand, and the price had risen to $1,800.

So-called Blacks were prominent as musicians in the Confederate Army. They were buglers, fifers, and drummers, many of whom history tells as **volunteers**. (Believe it or not.) (Mostly not.)

Hardtack biscuit was a dry heavy wafer made of flour and water. The North and South rationed them to their soldiers in which some used to thicken the consistency of soup.

Near the end of the Civil War, slaves in New Orleans were called **indentured servants**, mostly white children. (Edomites)

Newly captured Hebrew slaves in Africa were **licked to test the salt content** in their sweat. This would prove they might survive the long journey to America. (Refer to page 3)

Source: "Le commerce de l'Amerique par Marseille", engraving by Serge Daget, Paris 1725

Ouidah means Judah. It's a historical slave-trade city in Benin, West Africa. Hebrew slaves were captured from **Negroe Land** and shipped from its ports (Including Michael's ancestor.). (Page 94)

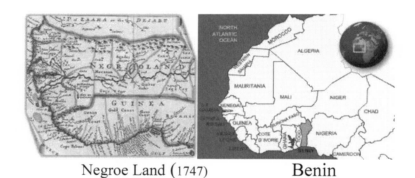

Negroe Land (1747)   Benin

Ouidah, Benin
(Monument is on Gulf of Guinea beachline.)

Door of No Return.

This book
Africa being an Accurate Description of the Region was created by John Ogilby
Printed in 1670
(Proves so-called Black Jews were on the West Coast of Africa.)

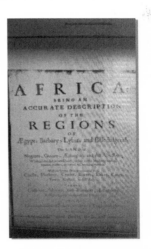

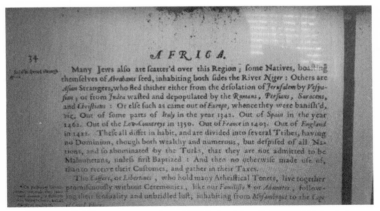

Page 34
(Transcription)

Many Jews also are scattered over this region, some **natives**, boasting themselves of *Abrahams* seed, inhabiting both sides of the River Niger: others are Asian Strangers, who fled thither either from the desolation of **Jerusalem** by Vespasian; or from Judea wasted and depopulated by the Romans.

Roman Invasion

In 66 A.D. the so-called Black Jews of Judea (Modern day Israel) rebelled against their occupying Roman masters. Emperor Nero later dispatched Vespasianus Augustus that commanded an army to crush the rebellion. As his legions advanced, almost a million Judean Hebrews fled, migrating great distances over time to the western and southern nations of Africa. *Mathew 24:16*

In 68 A.D. Nero committed suicide and Vespasianus became the new emperor of Rome. He later sends his son Titus to Judea in 70 A.D. and when his soldiers breached the city walls of Jerusalem, they began the slaughter and enslaving of thousands of remaining so-called Black Israelites including women and children. After the Romans confiscated relics from the temple that sat in the center of the city, the soldiers were ordered to burn it to the ground. The Jews cried in horror as black smoke rose above the entire under sieged city.

The Hebrews fought valiantly for three more years and were finally defeated. The remaining Jews in the country of Judea were either killed or put into Roman slavery. The prophecies in the bible had begun to come true. *1Kings 14:13, Deuteronomy 4:27*

Jerusalem

The real demolished city of *Jerusalem* (so-called Canaanite that was once ruled by Hamites) is near Tel Arad, south of Tel Aviv and to the west of the Dead Sea. There the *City of David* and *Mount Zion* are the same place. In misleading Tel Aviv, they are in two separate locations, *City of David* being low in a Valley on the southern slope of Mount Moriah and *Mount Zion* on the highest part of the Southwestern hill.

Jewish Imposters Origin

The Khazars (Russian white people) from the Caucasus region of Russia began converting the Hebrew religion (9th century) into their own, not wanting to be influenced by other countries. If they chose Orthodox Christianity they would fall under the influence of Byzantine Empire. If they chose Islam, they would've been under the influence of the Umayyads. They didn't know about the Hebrew teachings until so-called Black Jews traveled across the Balkan Peninsula.

Later, the Khazars were forced to convert to Judaism by John Hyrcanus, a High Priest and Hasmonean Leader that ruled from 134 to 104 BCE.

The Jewish people today called Ashkenazi originated from Eastern and Central Europe. Over the passing of years the population grew, migrating from Russia to Poland, Lithuania, Germany, and many other surrounding countries.

The Jewish Star of David has been around since 6000 BC and used by many cultures over the years like the German Swastika. 卐

It is believed that the star has been connected to (Remphan) false pagan worship. Moses had a hard time getting the people of Israel to denounce the symbol. The star has been called the *Shield of David* and the *Seal of Solomon*. It is not mentioned anywhere in the Bible.

In **1948**, the United Nations voted to allow Israel to be a Jewish state in the Middle East. Most so-called Black Israelites in America know that the country of Israel is in Africa including Egypt. After receiving a call from Washington, the Philippines casted the one deciding vote on UN resolution 181 that approved the imposters to become a country that governed itself. It was the only Asian country to vote yes. Because of this, no Filipino is required to have a Visa when entering the state of Israel. They shouldn't since they are actually part of the Lost Tribe of Levi. They gave away their own land not knowing they are the descendants of Levites. The Philippines which is the only Asian Christian nation, is mentioned in the Bible. Once called Ophir and rich with gold, it is written in the Old testament *1 Kings 22:48, 9:28*, and *22:4*.

Slaves in China

It is said online that so-called Black slaves built the Great Wall of China. It's not proven, but slaves were sold during the T'ang dynasty (960-1280 A.D.) from Persian envoys. The Chinese called the Israelites K'unlun. Also Marco Polo's relatives sold slaves to China when the opportunity was available.

First Black Pharaoh.
(Hamite)

In 730 B.C. a so-called Black Nubian king named Piye invaded the divided warlord ruled country of Egypt. He and his royal predecessors reigned over the country for almost 75 years. To celebrate Piye's death, he was awarded as being the first so-called Black pharaoh to be buried in an Egyptian style pyramid with two of his horses.

The Nubians who resided in which is now Sudan, brought gold to Egypt which was not common to the area. King Tut and Nefertiti which may have been his mother, were also part so-called Black. (Google)

DNA proves our heritage.
(E1B1A)

Moses was so-called black and mistakened as an Egyptian. King Ramsees 3rd carried the E1B1A haplotype gene.

(Jesus name, Hebrew Translation)

Ha Mashayach Yahawashi
(The Messiah Jesus Christ)

Revelation 1:14-15
14 The hair on his head was white like wool, as white as snow, and his eyes were like blazing fire.
15 His feet were like bronze glowing in a furnace, and his voice was like the sound of rushing waters.

Yahawashi (Jesus) died to save *only* the children of Israel from their sins (Acts 2:21-22). They are the descendants of Hebrews scattered all around the world which includes the so-called Black Americans, Hispanics, Native Americans and Seminole Indians.

King James 1611

Mathew 15:24   (Jesus spoke)
Acts 5:31
Isaiah 45:17
Romans 11:26-27

Mathew 1: 20-21

Amos 3:1-2 / Deuteronomy 28:68

I hope this book got your attention. It was written before I was awakened and I still think it is funny. But seriously, God is holding all of us (Israelites) accountable for following his laws and commandments. Don't wait before it's too late. The warning signs of Jesus's return are slowly being revealed. Your salvation and the breaking of the curse, is in your own hands.

Michael K. Jones

Become an Author and Screenwriter

Available on Amazon and Kindle

Learn to write and sell your own novel and screenplay.

This instruction manual has step by step instructions with sample pages to help you from beginning-to-end on how to complete your first novel.

It is also filled with information on how to write a screenplay. I've added website links that will help you find a literary agent including how to self-publish your book almost for free. Check out the sample pages of all my books on Amazon especially *Profiling or Prejudice*.

www.amazon.com

Made in the USA
Columbia, SC
15 March 2018